Differences

Di Hall

Published by Di Hall

Text Copyright © Di Hall 2016

Cover design by © Elizabeth Fitt

All rights reserved. No part of this publication may be reproduced, stored in a retrieval system, or transmitted in any form or by any means, electronic, mechanical, photocopy, recording or otherwise, without prior written permission of the copyright owner. Nor can it be circulated in any form of binding or cover other than that in which it is published and without similar condition including this condition being imposed on a subsequent purchaser.

British Library Cataloguing Publication Data.
A catalogue record for this book is available from the British Library

ISBN 978-0-9954728-0-8

Contents

Introduction	v
Prison	7
Travelling	13
The Burden Heavy.	18
The Ramblings and Experience	23
of Japan	23
Holding the Environment	35
In Sacrifice to Managements	42
The Ilusion And Disolusionment Of Change	42
Her name was Irene	51
Beyond Addiction	58
Conscience and Sensitivity	65
Abbie	72
Concluding	79

Introduction

The book raises the awareness of individual and group difference and how the wider context of politic and collective conscience affects our lives. It looks to the family and how that shapes us as individuals and how the powerful dramas of family life can be played out in work/social situations. It challenges us to look at our own self awareness and acceptance and questions, how can I accept another if I can't accept myself. It then goes on to talk about the authentic self and how this richness can affect us in our relationships with others.

The conclusion challenges our own attitudes and ingrained prejudices we hold against others who are different from ourselves. It recognises that many of us have been broken to pieces by non-empathic relationships and that this has left its scars. However it purports that the openness of our spirit at its core has profound healing and purpose. It argues that it is only the touch of God at the core of ones spirit that can authenticate true relationship to change lives.

Chapter 1

Difference

How can one begin to express in a paragraph of few words the colourful tapestry woven for the purpose of Gods creation. The deliberate intricate details sown together in a miracle for living life. A blend of pervasive colour, that brings creation alive. A mingling of blue and red. The compatibility of reason and respect. The very presence of compassion, acceptance and humility. For me the rainbows set in the skies represents God at peace, with one colour lingering upon the next creating a unity and discord of colour. A merge of richness and reflection that must touch the very heart of God. The matched and unmatched phenomenon of living alongside another.

I have often pondered upon the colours at dusk. The dimness of light that complements the artist's shaded areas of energy and inspiration. The talent that lies in the very nature of contrast and shading. A contrast of colours that represent diversity and polarity within the same pallet. A preparation of potential harmony, or a mixture of fragmentation and unrest. Whatever the blend of colour there lays the potential to split and divide. A divide that can emerge from suspicion and the fear of difference. A difference of culture, language, politic, ethnicity, individuality, personality and opinion. A difference that frustrates or complements, includes and excludes. It's the very difference that separates you from me.

In the journey of life I cultivated an inquisitiveness about the purpose and understanding of difference. I had so many unanswered questions that perhaps echo's some of your own. I became interested in the actual mix of differences. It brought my awareness to the edges of the paint, the line that divide's, the peripheries of life itself. In my investigation I began to look at the differences of social groupings, the dance it performs, its function and the merging and separation when life's pressures press in.

The study of social groupings has been a compelling insight into the fear and insecurity of being an insider and outsider. You will notice I have not assumed that being an insider promotes security. On the contrary being an insider or outsider maintains its own securities and dangers depending upon the situation, individuality, need, culture and social setting. Added to the dilemma is the contrast of personality and the nature of being introvert or extrovert. The introvert who is fearful of falling apart at the centre of self and the extrovert who is busy punctuating existence in fear of extinction. Whatever the nature both introvert and extrovert will ultimately be influenced by the social expectation of culture, family, grouping, race, religion or nationality.

It's intriguing the dynamic that occurs between any two individuals. It's a subjective entity that can act as a powerful and influential force. I remember experiencing the movement and dance whilst working within residential settings particularly when members joined and left the group. The group organism proved to be a powerful piece of machinery. It presented as a multi faceted and complex system that could both enable or disable. Culture, age, folklore, experience, race, mode, fad, politic, language and interpretation are but just a few aspects that taints its existence.

The family

Where better to begin than the family, from birth to death. One cannot divorce a family from its history. For example the family's past, present assumptions, beliefs, taboo, and the very unfolding nature of its pattern and ritual. The nature and nurture of family life is where relationship begins. You learn quickly in this environment about values and expectations, what I can do and what I can't. Family values and expectations are very emotive and probably the most influential forces that one might ever experience. From the extreme rigidity of control to a nurture of passivity. The intricacies of family life and its complexities gives birth to a system of dynamics be it functional or dysfunctional. For example the drama of the dyad, disengagement, enmeshment and triangulation's. All of these dynamics set up the stage for different roles to be played out i.e. puppets, ventriloquists, scapegoats and ghosts. The frightening fact is that the roles played often become dysfunctional in necessitating the whole. Often families are not aware that they are feeding into the maintenance of such dramas. Do you recognise what relationship in the family support's your symptom?

A parent's job is a hardy employment and one that always falls short of perfection. But what positions do parents hold? Magnified figures in the backdrop of our minds yielding reeves of peace and persuasion. Are we able to understand the bond and attachment we have with our parents will? A will that attempts to idealise and turn you into something you're not. The rescuer after all is lost; the persecutors and victims of all proceeding thought and action. Our parents wills. The purest intention and the extension of ourselves. The ultimate product of their wishes desires and fantasies. Their dreams of unfulfilled and ambitions tightly gripped in vain that they might fall away. Winnicott (1987 p70) so adequately identifies with this and quotes'

'Moreover the forces at work in determining the behaviour

both of the parents and of the child are so hidden with foundations so deep in the unconsciousness, that intellectual attempts to modify events resemble the scratching of initials on the pillars of a cathedral…………they do little more than reflect the conceit of the artist.'

Do you remember all those fears as a child hiding away from the unknown and unexplained? The fears of phantom and ghost. Being on the edge of cliffs and crossing bridges. Do you remember the fear you possessed when punishment was due, the shame and disgrace that clawed away at your soul. The fears of getting it right, of getting it wrong, accompanied by the oppression of silence. Much of what is learnt in the family is indelible and inevitably acted out in many other social groups and settings. It's what I refer to as the present past. The only escape from some of the more damaging and repetitive patterns begins with self awareness. I often chuckle when people refer to other people's baggage from the past when they themselves fall short of their own introspection. We are all subjects of baggage, unique in experience and value.

I quake at the times I have unconsciously re-enacted family roles when under pressure. This inevitable disturbance can unconsciously portray itself in joint efforts of professional intervention and project. As a ploy I have often hid behind professionalism, given my practise approach a name and hoped for the best. I learnt not to give too much time or listen to hard to detail. Pressed against time I've utilised avoidance, kept my distance, thrown money at situations of complexity, referred affairs to other professionals and said nothing to everything. I don't know a professional who has not at some stage resulted to such practises. It's a devise of covering your back, ducking and diving from the contagion and sieges of poverty, distress, and the sometimes-impossible demands upon relationship.

How do we experience family and group situation? Do they inspire, challenge and above all facilitate or are they the dread of all that we have become. I believe it begins with a good awareness and concept of self; the acceptance of self as well as others; and a wide understanding of the effects and implications of external forces. If I am not able to accept myself as I am how can I ever begin to accept another? This awareness and acceptance of self goes far beyond the differences of nature race and culture. It runs at a depth level of humanity, spiritual awareness and understanding. The mastery of developing such awareness and acceptance lies in the journey of life. It's an arduous journey of continually being open to all challenges and opportunities in the renewal of self and our relationships with others. A lack of self-acceptance and awareness will almost always results in the potentiality of discriminating against another. There are many shadows that lie deep within the subconscious, awaiting their chance of submergence. Under pressure the layered efforts of disguise often fall away and for moments at a time reveal our naked natures. Being open to ourselves in this way is probably the hardest journey of all. Without doubt the true complexes begin when we risk being open and honest with ourselves and others.

Within the passage of time I have learnt to live within the paradoxes of life i.e. the understanding of a war created in the effort for peace; the division of a group for the purpose of pollination; the splitting of the individual self in search of truth. Where light breaks through the eye of darkness, and rests its reason. It all starts with a sense of curiosity and search for purpose and reason. The stepping inside and outside of oneself in curiosity. Literally getting outside of the goldfish bowl to examine what is going on. I recall an Indian proverb that states,

'the last creature that is aware of the sea is the fish'.

It's quite amusing how subservient we have become to society unaware of a greater and powerful creator. How we are trained and developed throughout the years to serve industrial mechanisms of power, politic and capital. It's not surprising that the saturation of man/woman's influence and product gets in the way of the search for spiritual awareness, and the intimate relationship with a more powerful protector. Within the these fictional tales there are some fascinating and descriptive accounts of individual relationships in some very different settings. The stories focus upon the quality of relationships made. It touches upon the divide of nature and being, and searches the heart for a deeper level of understanding of our relationship one with another. What a sad affair if we cannot be touched by adversity and the anguish of suffering. Take time to be effected by these privileges as this true God begins to shape us for his purposes. These humorous and sometimes sad stories told might be something you are able to relate to, so sit tight as I attempt to bring these characters alive.

Chapter 2

Prison

Loitering once behind prison walls the experience of group living and survival hit Joanne hard. The core of the group was brutal, raw and held by the toughest of gay females. Persons wanting to affiliate or register recognition needed to be able to act and pace out their reputations. Misfits, and hanger on's were not easily tolerated and were eventually forced into performing menial tasks of shinning shoes, folding clothes, making beds and sexual chores. These tasks carved out an existence for the vulnerable and insecure. It was a devious ploy of making other inmates subservient to a crude system of power. One quickly learnt the rules of the 'pac'. The hardest task was holding onto the sense of self whilst living alongside the façade presented by inmates. Many women broke under the pressure of divided allegiance. The secret was keeping oneself to oneself without mental, emotional or physical weakness seeping out at the seams. A relative descriptive state for survival would be that of the hollow woman, as hard as nails and clinically approved of when under pressure.

Clipping Joannes wings to join such a setting was something she could never have predicted. Many of the days were passed counting the minuets and hours. However, Joanne was fortunate enough to have been placed on the hospital wing. The hospital wing was the safest environment in this establishment. Existing alongside others in their frailties would excuse her from the expectation of joining ranks with the general mob. The only draw back was the exposure to some of the saddest and maddest of individuals.

The system of control in these establishments is very apparent and friendships aren't easily made. Revenge is sweet within these walls. Rage and violence can erupt in seconds and die down as though nothing had ever taken place. Other subtle revengeful actions of indiscriminate urination, spitting and the wetting up of beds were prevalent. Contaminated food and other unexpected surprise's were ways of sending messages of warnings. The subtler it was the better. In that way no one could add days to a sentence for affairs unproven.

Several acquaintances with inmates came to Joannes mind on looking back. A young girl aged fourteen named Beth was placed in the same hospital wing as Joanne. She presented as a quiet, unassuming character. At an early age she had been given up for adoption and grew up with what she referred to as a missing part. Her behaviour was marred by insecurities. In desperate ploys for attention she would change into a camellia, absorbing and drawing energy from anyone and everyone at hand. Despite forming a good relationship with Beth there were times when Joanne could barely connect or recognise her. Beth had no allegiance to anyone or anything and was only compelled by her own need for attention. This in turn was swayed by her changing mood and emotion that would spill over into self-harm. She was like a time bomb waiting to go off, totally vulnerable and volatile to the environment. Her sense of truth was in some ways refreshing however she had no sense of reason or fear. Joanne would often watch her chaotic sense of self-weave in and out of different situations of the day. An innocent babes in arms surviving in the only way she knew how. Joanne consistently kept her at a safe distance. She adopted a robotic unemotional approach that would protect her. In fact in essence, basic animal behaviour was a necessity, acting and pacing out unspoken boundaries was essential. Despite maintaining a hard exterior Joannes heart would melt in response to Beths antics and games played . Joanne knew that no one human being would ever have enough love to give her.

Many hours were spent locked up due to staffing issues and the politics of prison life. Boredom chipped away at the soul and at the senseless waste of time. Games of amusement were created to fill this valuable time. Catching live flies in a tooth box container was one of the favourites. With rules attached it proved to be a game of precision and nerve. Stimulation and occupation of the mind and body was essential to keep going. Being lost in the presence of the moment tended to have the opposite effect of awaiting time to past towards release dates. There was enough time to think about this. There was also enough time to ruminate upon the broken past; the loss of loved ones, partners, children, homes, possessions, health and life itself.

Joanne goes on to describe another woman named Annie whom she met up with everyday in the workroom. Joannne says that she was loud, foul-mouthed, and very crude. The sort of character that was in your face demanding agreeable responses. Joanne could hear her now ruling with an intrusive context of trivialities. If given eye contact she would hold you to ransom the whole morning matching the approval of her own self-opinionated humour and jest. She was constantly there in the background of affairs, the soap queen begging an audience. Her vulgar insinuations were penetrating. Joanne found it difficult to smile in the acknowledgement of her presence. She became an object to avoid at all costs, until one day Joanne noticed that she couldn't hear her any more. She was there but in total silence. Astonished at the radical change Joanne began to enquire of others about the cause. One inmate took Joanne aside and said, 'she's Beth's mother, but Beth doesn't know it yet. She hasn't seen her since giving her up at birth'.

It was the crudest of reunions ever, something that only happens in the soap's. The distinguishing factor of identity had originated from a double barrelled sir name they had in common. Beth was oblivious to the discovery. Annie was so shocked that she was reduced to a pulp, an empty shell drained of content. Joanne watched on as Annie tipped toed around Beth examining her in every detail. It was like a dog with a lost pup. Beth's eventual reaction to the news appeared neutral. Her behaviour never changed other than a hesitant caution she adopted in the presence of her newly found mother.

It felt strange that in the twentieth century that such an affair might occur without sensitive intervention. Joanne was so touched over such an incident it tore back the layers of judgement she had held about the characters involved. So much time driven between these individuals and yet drawn together in the tide of enlightenment and cruel circumstance. The kiss of reunification, the horror, denial, shame, and unexpected joy, falling through a moment in time. What a curious and unexpected event Joanne was so privileged to witness.

Joanne thought upon the variety of women that lived within these walls. Many of the them should never have been incarcerated. It was as though the world had severely judged their ailments, disabilities, in-abilities and poverty. Mary was one such character. Fragile in mental health she was unable to curb her kleptomania. Plastic knifes lighters and matches were just a few of her fads. She spent many hours alone and looking on in silence. Her muted existence haunted the backdrop of group living. Lorraine on the other hand was affluent, financially secure and well educated. Lorraine had been imprisoned for burgling a private and occupied dwelling. She had dressed up as a man in order to achieve her endeavour. After only two days she was transferred from the block to the hospital wing and then removed and put on a section for her own safety. What happened you may ask? The power of affluence cannot buy into relationships that exist in these establishments. Her endeavours to rule and reign with affluence and riches came to a violent and abrupt end. Inmates here rule with tough respect and a crude sense of genuinity and justice. There is no sense of favour or bribery if it doesn't fit the occasion. Some women here have nothing to loose. The emotional pain borne from the past has been so much so that physical pain is nought and not an issue. You have to have been scarred to walk safely within these walls.

Joanne thought upon her own experience within theses walls. Prisons are not places for the faint hearted even although the walls are packed with the sick and poor. That's not to say that amongst inmates there are not those that are just bad. However the most intentional and meticulous of criminals represents just a small average. Most of the inmates have injustices stacked against their existence. Some have not been able to control themselves or their sicknesses and in response have surrendered themselves to the walls of these buildings. Some have nothing to gain from living in society and have made their homes within these same walls. What is it that is so attractive to being held captive and being subject to a rule of regulation? For some it might be the only refuge of security ever felt or the only space where one is safe from oneself.

When one looses their freedom one looses a certain amount of control over ones existence. It robs the mind of itself, choice, reason, thought and will. Freedom as such does not exist in this sense. However with control handed over to others there is no reason to think for tomorrow because it is already held, secure and will look after itself. Power and control is an awesome subject and in the wrong hands can be both oppressive and perverse. In such establishments of prison it is raw and evident. It demands subservience and particularly effect's the behaviour of the most vulnerable. Bowing and begging being the crudest of behaviours. It gives license to predators and victims. It rips away at the layers of self and exposes insecurities.

The confinement of space inevitably forces one to escape through the pockets of ones mind. Conviction, fantasy and dreams then take over and become a source of release. For Joanne the time and space permitted an escape into solitude in which she developed a more reflective attitude. This permitted space was essential. She experienced it as a curious stage in which she opened to self and questioned her very existence. It provided a valuable prelude to thought and action. It paused and impregnated foresight and was central to a spiritual awakening and understanding for the living of life. The confined space of prison for Joanne was probably the easiest space in which to get lost in fantasy the most valuable space in which to be falsely converted; and yet in spiritual solitude it presented itself as the most holy and truest space of all.

Chapter 3

Travelling

During seven years of travelling as an artist Sofie was once contracted to a small village in Belgium. At this point in time working away from home was getting more and more difficult. The distance and time away from family, friends and her son was too painful to describe. Sofie and her son share the suffering marks of separation and loss. The severing of bond and attachment had had much influence in their relationship. Time lost between individuals tends to scar the heart and never makes up for the true investment of growing together. Although one can never go back to live the past one can learn from our children's reactions and change the future of what is to be. Sofies son would always remind her that one day they would be together. With that thought in mind she ventured out again into yet another contract this time in the small village of Boutersem.

Sofie remembers arriving at Ostend where she was met by the Padron, Leanda. Leanda was a stunning blond standing over six-foot tall. She was as elegant in her dress as she was in her over played mannerisms. She had a wide and striking smile balanced against refined and petite features of nose, chin and cheekbones. Her eyes were delicately slanted up and out similar to that of an Egyptian Queen. She was a picture of beauty. Her colleague by the name of Kelly trotted along after her as though in total obedience. Kelly smiled at Sofie tentatively after scrutinising her every part.

Leanda peered down at Sofie and in an abnormally deep voice said 'You must be Sofie'. Sofie looked twice to check that the voice was coming from the same person. With very little effort Leanda hurled up Sofies baggage and bundled it in the back of a car and added, 'You'll do'. Her neck was that of a swallow with the most abnormally protruding adam's apple that Sofie had ever seen on any female. A quick flurry of thoughts made Sofie hesitate and wander what she had signed up to. Sofie thought it's times like this when one wants to telephone the Agent and demand he get you out of here.

The owner of the establishment where Sofie was to commence her contract was a seventy-year-old Belgium man, who appeared uninterested in the running of the business. He was a picture of belligerence and spent most of the time sitting in the kitchen beside his shotgun, drinking coffee. He spoke only Flemish and understood little English. He would very occasionally look up to acknowledge Sofies existence, nod and say, 'ok'? Leanda was very intimate and blasé with the old man, sometimes to the point of bullying. Sofie never knew what was being constantly argued over between the two and was never to find out the genuine connection or relationship between them.

Sofie detected a very strong allegiance between Leanda and her colleague Kelly. She couldn't make out to what level this relationship had been tested, but knew at once that she wouldn't even be considered as a part of this duo, even as a colleague. It was a closed relationship with all outsiders barred from entry.

It wasn't like any other place Sofie had been contracted to before and it was the first time she had ever worked so closely with transsexuals. When Sofie was with them together the relationship between them became exhaustive and competitive. The interaction was stilted and false as though being played out for an audience. Some days were worse than others with the continued drama eating away at life itself. The emotion invested in the dramas played often ended up in some of the most bizarre and extravagant behaviours. However, the stage and performance for Sofie ended at 5.00am each morning, when she was ready to lead, as best she could, a normal existence. It was her way of survival. It wasn't long before Sofie decided to dis-identify with her colleagues and spend less time alongside. She was truly an outsider who had earned the name as 'granate' taken from the name of pomegranate, the fruit of many seeds.

At the earliest opportunity Kelly took Sofie to one side and explained that Leanda's capricious moods and dramas were due to an intolerable imbalance of hormone medication. Kelly endeavoured to protect Sofie from some of Leanda worst temperaments as well as from her own. Sofie was touched by such consideration.

Over the days and months Sofie got to know Kelly very well. During that time she disclosed an exceptionally sad and emotionally tortured past as a child. Kelly remembers being teased and ridiculed as a male from an early age. Preferential affection was poured upon the fairer sex of her two sisters who she grew up to admire and envy. Kelly's mother was a methodical character who had little tolerance for the male species of this world. Her time was taken up with business achievements and her feminist companions. Kelly's father had left the home when she was just two months. The marriage had been like a roller coaster and was deemed to fail. Subsequently Kelly was to loose the most important link to the role model of male existence.

Kelly shared many stories of confusion of her sex and the shame of her genitals. As a youngster she would spend many hours watching her sisters grooming and receiving verbal affirmation from their mother. It wasn't long before Kelly began cross-dressing at the early age of twelve. She would spend an enormous amount of time looking at her reflection in order to change characteristics and mannerisms to that of a female. Adolescence proved to be a very difficult period of isolation and fear. The shame and confusion over gender identity became so intolerable that she began abusing herself in some very inconceivable ways. By the age of sixteen Kelly had left home and in the years to follow she lost all contact with friends, family, and alternatively became a recluse. At the age of twenty-one Kelly met someone who was to change her life. She quotes, 'He picked me up from nothing and demanded nothing. He helped to clothe me appropriately and put me into accommodation that was secure. He totally accepted me for who I was and imbued into me a sense of worth and confidence'. This was probably the most settling period of Kelly's life

Kelly's friend was to support her through a lengthy period of five years whilst she changed her gender. It was a long agonising period of visiting medics and psychiatrists. Kelly commented how this companionship had stabilised her in a hard-nosed battle to discover her chosen identity. She quotes with words to the affect, 'from an unworthy depraved wretch who was closed in on self I began to discover the world as though for the first time. It took someone who was prepared to give me a true reflection of my situation and circumstance to pull me through. Someone with the audacious patience of a saint to tolerate the unruly nature of character and mood. From a bottomless pit I took a risk and trusted in someone willing to listen in silence. Someone who was un-condemning, selfless and un-judgemental. There are but a few, but my friend was one of those characters. I guarded him secretly and kept him securely locked in the box of my soul. This friendship was not for sharing or comparing and remains the secret lock to my existence and being'.

Sofies heart melted with compassion on hearing Kelly's story. She was taken back by the level of honesty and openness entrusted. In response her own sexual identity loomed before her reminding her of how much she took for granted. She couldn't begin to imagine what it would be like being a female ensnared within a male body. Her world was so protected from anything out side such a tragedy. What a smug individual I am thought Sofie, so entrenched within the normality's of culture and creed. If only she could cut out a piece of herself and give it to Kelly. Sofie thought on how her relationship with Kelly must have provoked the memory of a detached existence with her siblings. Memory has such a powerful way of intruding upon relationships in this way.

Sofie realised how world's apart they were in purpose and being. Two separate entities flung together in a small moment of time with absolutely nothing in common other than an urgent need of capital. How could Sofie possibly empathise with such a situation? Towards the end of the contract Kelly looked at Sofie and requested that she sleep with her. Sofie immediately froze as a flurry of thoughts flooded her head. She was aghast at what to say. She remembers stumbling and bumbling over the words, 'I wouldn't know what to do Kelly'! Kelly just smiled and added, 'I just want to be close to you, nothing more'. It was a response that alerted Sofie to just another human being, hurting and hungry for comfort.

Its instances like these that suddenly remind you of the small mindedness of perception. How and when do we ever grow out of the prejudices of traditional thought, the gripping prisms of the 'norm' and the belief systems of historical past? What learning we have to achieve to maximise understanding alone.

Chapter 4

The Burden Heavy.

It had been sometime since Sharon checked in with anyone about her whereabouts. She didn't know whether jumping bail was such a good idea but it presented such a precious opportunity of travelling abroad with the troop of dancers she'd met. Her plan was always to give herself up when she returned but at this immediate moment in time she needed respite and time out to think about her plight. She was so in angst that she would receive a prison sentence this time around. Having her wings clipped and loosing freedom posed the ultimate threat to life itself. On the other hand the opportunity of travelling to Italy and the experience of sun, pasta and wine posed as a more favourable option. The memory leading to this event was so vivid in her mind. At the time life had become chaotic. The steady stream of substances that kept her life together had dried up and she was falling apart. Three days clear of substance and she was already beginning to merge with reality it wouldn't be long before her emotion would lie bear and her sense of humour would rage as though in birth. What could she do to subdue this passing tide? The vacuous space of her existence needed to be filled until the next pick-up. Alas, three days into detoxification and she finds herself being arrested and charged with burglary. In a state of flux she pleaded guilty to everything they wished to charge her with for the sake of sanity and freedom. She had tread this path before and was only too aware of the system she was now caught up in.

She recalled the incident so well. It was midday and the sun was beating down. Many visitors had called at the door in a similar state but this time bringing with them a set of associates that she wasn't so familiar with. Sharon knew that when sources dried up your acquaintances and opportunities became unlimited and if you weren't careful your sudden state of consciousness could easily be influenced by the wrong source. One of Sharon's callers was a character who she had seen around for a number of years but had not until now had any interaction with. He didn't fit into any one group of associates. She remembers him as always being on the periphery of affairs, a character that was always at the scene of a crisis, but never part of it, like a buzzard on the fringe of its prey. Sharon recalls thinking, what is he wanting here. She had no investment of relationship with him. He had nothing to bargain with or anything of value to offer. In her minds eye she had him tabbed, and labelled with reservation. At a glance he must have known what Sharon was thinking because he suddenly asserted himself and asked her if she would like to visit what he described as an abandoned home. The visit would be to her gain as there were many household goods to be had. His interjection saved him from an instant judgement of worthlessness. Was this creature of value after all and might Sharon give him the opportunity to prove his credibility.

They both arrived at the abandoned house just after 2.00pm. Sharon remembers it well the sun was still very hot and there was a distinct scent of lavender in the air. The house was huge and set back from the main road. Sharon became suddenly curious about the previous inhabitants and probed her companion for more information about the occupant's whereabouts. 'No, he exclaimed, there's no one living here any longer. They've all departed. Its not the first time I have visited.' As they approached the porch Sharon could see the front door wide open through to the reception area. They climbed the porch steps entered through the front door and into a grand hallway. The hallway led off into various different rooms that were decadently furnished and carpeted. Others had obviously visited before them as there was an array of items strewed across the floor. Sharon suddenly felt uneasy and beckoned that they leave however her companion was at complete ease and in complete confidence began to rummage amongst the abandoned bric a brac. It was in the contagion of that confidence that Sharon relaxed and began to search her surroundings. However whilst collecting some mugs and packing them up in a basket they were instantly affronted by two police officers, arrested, and charged with burglary. Sharon was taken aside searched and handcuffed to her associate who in turn had all his clothes taken away. He clutched onto a blanket in attempts to cover his nudity. In the midst of Sharon's dilemma, thoughts of total submission came to mind. Why had she allowed herself to be in the wrong place at the wrong time and now to be tied to a wretch of a being whose idea it was in the beginning? In vengeance the thought of doing a runner and trailing him in his entirety brought a slight smile to her lips. A daring sense of the bazaar exhumed her and she could hardly hold herself back. In her mind she was now running down the road at a rate of knots dragging with her a nude figure of a man. Hands clasped together she yanked him over the terrain of fields and thistle. With abated breath he begs her to slow down. However, with her own goal fixed firmly in mind she barely hears his pleas, after all this is a mission of liberation and at all costs. Sharon's attachment now battered and in a state of poor repair begins to lug behind. The weight becomes heavy and she gradually grinds to a halt. In a moment of frustration and anger droplets of perspiration begin to trickle from her brow. How could she be seen as associating with such a character? What would others say, how would she begin to explain? Maybe she could explain her plight as an accident, an experiment that was beyond her control. No, that wouldn't ware. Oh my goodness she could see the headlines now, 'Escaped Road Runner closely pursued by a Naked Attachment'. She could read the flurry of thoughts flowing through their minds, the sniggers and expressions in response. There was no rational explanation she had been caught out in her own sad judgement and her own credibility was now at stake. In retaliation and disgust she glared upon his frailty. Maybe she could subject his calamity to her own rules and regulations. Oh dear, such power ripples away at the glee felt. A sense of grandiose grips her as she now towers above his petty frame. Conquered foe and slave for whatever purpose she chose. A powerful image recalled with such clarity. However, on second thought this might mistakenly be interpreted as a longstanding relationship. The sudden image of a life long commitment alerts a dreaded fear and then a desperate sense of despair rises up and fixates her in thought. What if she was chained to him for life never to sense her own solitude ever again? She began to envisage pulling this creature around in sickness and health, till death do us part, until flesh departs. What if he was to die and she was expected to carry his rotting body around until it decayed. She could hardly say she never knew him. It would be a living tomb draped with guilt and shame about her own being. Perhaps she could cut him off or ignore him; pretend he wasn't there, like a figment from imagination. That is hardly unlikely as he has been hung onto her by metal pins. An everlasting body deemed to follow her wherever she might go. If she were to project the anger of her fate upon anyone it would be on him. Might she ever learn to have compassion upon this human wretch? Sharon shuddered at the thought and as she glanced at him she became overwhelmed with contempt and once again all rationale was lost. This time Sharon is running after him equipped with mallet and cleave ready to commit murder. The smell of his fear propels her forward in pursuit. She is now in range and just about to complete the kill when she is suddenly alerted to, 'and if you have anything to say it will be written down and given in evidence'.

In Reflection

Rekindling the incident raises many issues for Sharon. Let's look at the instant totality of judgement made about this character. The judgement goes far beyond the categorisation of personality or status; it encompasses his very worth of being. Already condemned to exclusion he would need to prove his right of belonging in thought action and deed. In fact to prove his allegiance he will need to bear his very soul. This poor creature has little chance of escaping the ascribed image drawn up in mind. He is prejudiced by assumption stacked upon assumption. Whatever is to happen in this tale he is surely deemed to fail in his efforts. He will always full short in expectation. His existence and presence is already in question and being measured up against investment and gain. He remains a non-player. He has lost before starting and will always remain under the eye of suspicion and scrutiny. Approval cannot be earnt. He will be used for gain but never acknowledged, recognised or respected within the perimeters of wider circles. Despite being given an opportunity to prove his credibility it will only be won for an instant before once again taking up his position as a failed outsider. What an impossible position to be in knowing that you will never be accepted whatever you accomplish, offer or sacrifice.

Chapter 5

The Ramblings and Experience of Japan

A six-month contract is in the pipeline this time in Japan. With my son at the heart of my calling I decide to take it. Six months of capital would go towards a home. The separation and departures are always so painful that I long to stay at home. My son detects the sadness and comforts me. I visualise the time when we will one day be together and begin to smile with him. The next moment I recall is flying off from Heathrow with tears drops running the length of my cheeks. I strain in my seat just to catch one more glimpse of family before settling down to the journey before me.

I was curious as to my choice of travelling to Japan I could have chosen to go anywhere other than to this Eastern Country. I thought upon my father's imprisonment as a Japanese prisoner of war and the silence of his experience within family life. Was this choice an attempt to trace the historical incidence or just a curious probe into the culture and mentality of those that had brutalised him? Or perhaps it was an attempt to get near his pain that had had no expression over the years. Would I return to England to share similar ideas with him about the values and characteristics of these people? Would it free him up in expression and hook up under the silence he guarded so well.

Would we at long last be able to share something in common or would it drive us even further away from one another in opposition. Am I chasing a solution to which there is no answer, only to leave me knocking hard on the door of forgiveness, or am I just chasing my own felt loss of a fathers love. Many thoughts crowd my mind as I prepare myself to being a stranger in a host country. I am already holding deep prejudices against my hosts and to what extent is yet unknown. The experience of my stay will hopefully challenge the intergenerational horror of war and the aftermath it has upon family life. Perhaps this is a chance of dismantling the hidden resentments of unhealed scars and opportunity to absolve the fragments of hurt felt.

On arriving in Tokyo the gestures of welcome by my hosts was ingratiating. After a short introduction they took my bags and I was driven to a hotel in the heart of Tokyo. This hotel was a central meeting point for Europeans. When you weren't working under contract you returned to this same hotel and if you were in luck of time and schedule you were sometimes able to meet up with friends. Tokyo is a busy city with building stacked upon building either side of the road. The streets are so alike and systematically laid out that it's not difficult to get lost. Getting lost was a dilemma I managed to experience on more than one occasion. Tokyo comes alive at night with its neon signs lit up on every corner and above every café and business. Wherever there's a space there's a business humming away in the background. In the backdrop of dusk I watch the workers as they go through their rituals of dance and movement before changing shift, a regular routine that is meant to strengthen the spirit de core before any work commences.

Everything was tightly organised and always on schedule whether it was arranged transport, flight or hotel, anything less was seen as chaos. This was a theme that ran throughout the culture, as well as the strong sense of servitude to any one cause. At each destination of contract I was met, greeted and taken to my accommodation. However once you had been taken to your accommodation and had dispensed with the rituals of departure you were left alone for days and weeks at a time unable to converse with anyone in your own language. I remember my journey as being a very lonely experience. The days were long and I felt at the mercy of time. Fortunately I spent the first month with a Japanese Theatre Company at a Hotel in Bandai near Fukushima. I was placed there with a young Brazilian woman whom I got to know well despite a hindering language barrier. I can see her now in my minds eye sitting for hours at a time sewing one sequin at a time on her costumes. There was a sense of grace with her every movement. I wondered what fate had chosen her profession and driven the time between herself and her homeland. We spent many hours together in silence and gesture. It was in our broken communication and understandings that I learnt much about her home life, friends, family and the extremes of poverty experienced. We both knew that this life would earn more than enough money to ease the poverty experienced. We also knew that money would only ever be objective in meeting need. It held little value in comparison to the driven purpose and meanings that affected both of our lives.

I remember one memorable night when I awoke to pounding on my bedroom door and shouts of sheer distress. I opened the door to find my Brazilian friend in a state of frenzy. Tears were rolling down the side of her cheeks as she attempted to explain her fear. I stepped aside and she rushed into the room. With a crucifix in one hand she was now kneeling down on her knees praying in hurried undertones of Spanish. She stretched out her hand to me as though retrieving life itself. Completely bemused by the event I decided that she had gone completely mad and was wondering what to do next when I felt the whole building move under my feet. I quickly scanned the room and noticed previous cracks running up the full length of the walls. A sudden panic gripped me. Was this going to be the time for the walls to erupt and divide? At this point she is not alone on her knees. I am now knelt opposite and with our arms now wrapped around one another we await our destiny. Whole minuets pass by as we clutch to one another. A feeling of not wanting to be alone in death took its course. Wherever my friend was destined I would be there alongside. I don't ever remember a sense of difference between myself and my friend at that moment in time. In fact an alarming sense of unity gripped me as nature groaned away and took its course. With one foot in the grave I awaited the next movement from beneath. However, when nothing occurred and time passed so my sense of being slowly returned. My flesh alerted itself and I began to peer out from between our folded arms. A sense of calm hit the air. In great relief I dropped to the side of my friend in sheer astonishment. I was aghast at the peace that had suddenly thrown us back into existence. With very few words of understanding between us we began comforting one another, embracing one another and smiling with relief. At that instance two Japanese hotel workers knocked at the door to serve tea and change the bedding as though nothing had ever occurred. My friend looked at me in shock and amazement. It was as though we had passed through a time warp with our hosts completely oblivious to what had passed. In response I shrugged my shoulders and we began to laugh together. It was the beginning of good friendship. During my stay in Japan I went on to experience several such common occurrences but I look back on this one with a smile at heart. It's alarming how our nature subsides in light of earth's wrath. That's what is so interesting about the tides of crisis and the opportunities it brings. It was from this moment onwards that the allegiance with my Brazilian friend grew towards one another and for the first time in weeks there was a sense of not being alone in a distant land. With an attuned awareness of discrimination we were able to share and comfort one another over some of the incidents that alienated us as Westerners. Together we battled with the difference of Japanese culture; we experimented with chopsticks, learnt the basics of the Japanese language and familiarised ourselves with expected rituals. In gestures of friendships our hosts became more familiar with us as strangers and came closer to inspect our eyes and touch our skin. They reached to feel the texture of our hair as though to check its authenticity, and then with one hand graciously covering their mouths they would giggle, timidly. We were so very different from our counterparts, fastidiously so in nature and appearance.

Compared with other countries Japan is probably the one place where I can say that I never ever got to know one Japanese person well. They were so apt at applying different mannerisms and personas for any one occasion. Their lives appeared to be so pre destined and systemised. It was as though the whole nation had been processed and churned out in mass. Even the underground tubes were rife in the organisation of its commuters with many of its passengers packed in the smallest of spaces like sardines. Hired men with white gloves were employed to literally push as many people on to the underground trains as possible. In service to industry everyone had a part to play. In the retail business there were people to take your money, people to wrap what you had purchased, and people to give you your change. It was all so very unnecessary I thought. The nature of chaos is probably the antithesis to this culture, or perhaps one of the same, being that they are opposites! In Japan it's not good to be seen doing anything outside the traditional norm as it only serves to disrupt and create fear and anxiety. So therefore everything that breathes has a sense of true order. With this in mind my friends based back in Tokyo were often up for challenging and upsetting the rhythmic pattern of Japanese life. In charades set up to alarm they were often up to their tricks selecting their next Japanese victims. Unfortunately their victims often turned out to be personnel from the hotel who in response would either hide, run away, or drop to the floor with their hands covering their heads.

In reflection the only sort of chaos and disorder that I witnessed in Japanese society was the very occasional street vagabond living in the streets. It was a rare sighting but all the same evident. During my stay I sighted just three in all. In fact if you weren't careful you would miss them with a single glance thinking it was just a heap of rubbish on the sidewalk. It's only the slow movement of swaddling bands that cause one to stop, look again and wonder. It was impossible to detect the flesh of hand face, feet of these characters as they were flushed against the camouflage of coverings consisting of layers and layers of torn rags. It was an intriguing sight watching them move against the flow of fast moving commuters in the high street. Their existence appeared to represent everything that was opposite to Japanese culture and lifestyle. A 'no one' existing nowhere, banished from society and possibly from themselves.

However, on the theme of chaos I do remember some of my own natural disasters that caused more than enough concern during my travels. One of these episodes was when I was travelling up the Shinkensen line on my way to Kyoto. I remember feeling tired during my journey and took everything to stay awake. The train was smooth running with almost no rhythmic sensation to its movement. Kyoto was now the seventh stop away, where I would hopefully be met by a courier. I remember everything up until the fifth stop. Whilst watching the coming and going of commuters and the foot vendors selling food along the platform I recall the figures merging into one another and it wasn't long before I was entering the dreams of oblivion. I suddenly awoke to urgent rapping on the outside of the window. I looked out to see a little man jumping up and down at a rate of knots in sheer desperation. It didn't dawn on me until seconds later that he was alerting me to some kind of catastrophe. By this time I had several interested parties gathered around me with great interest, all of whom were smiling. Everyone smiles in Japan. As the train eased off from the station I looked out of the window to see a little man smiling, in between bowing, and now running alongside the train. Oh dear I'd lost the plot and the stop. He continued to wave at me in an urgent fashion however it was too late; I was off to another destination. By now he was running faster than the train and I became a little concerned as to his performance. I remember looking back to see this figure still running after the tail end of the train. In a gesture of acknowledgement I raised my hand and gave him a slight wave. On reaching the end of the platform he raised his hands to his head as though in prayer to the Gods. It was just fifteen minuets to the next stop where a common occurrence happened. I woke again to a second knocking at the window. Did I manage to get off? Well yes, my second courier must have been well informed about the sleepy state of this European woman. I must say that it felt like a crisis well managed and with ease.

Another similar incident happened when I was awaiting a flight to the Isle of Kochi. However, this time it was me who was left running the length of a runway. I had been waiting a long time in the lobby and there was not a sign of any air traffic or evidence of passengers. A few people drifted into the waiting area but only to disappear after twenty minuets or so. A little agitated I walked the length of the room pacing in time to my innate nature. They couldn't have got this wrong. The flight I mean. They were all so pre-planned and organised. Suddenly, I hear the mention of Kochi Island but am not sure. I strain my ears again but hear nothing. The few people beside me gather up their bags and disappear. I wonder whether to approach them just to check that the plane was on schedule. I restrain myself apprehensively thinking that it would just be another performance of ritual and trying to make myself understood. Now, totally on my own I begin to wonder if it's possible that I am the only passenger travelling today. Egomania creeps in as I ponder on the idea of being the sole party in this aircraft. During the smugness of thought I am suddenly alerted to the mention of Kochi coming through the intercom system. Looking out through the full length windows of the lobby I see a huge aircraft manoeuvring itself into place in preparation of take off. With grace it eased itself towards the lobby and then turned full circle. And then it all happened. An air steward came running into the lobby asked to see my ticket and said, 'your plane is taking off, come'. Pleading for me to follow her she broke out into a run and urged me to follow. Both of us are now running along the runway in an attempt to catch up with the moving monster in front of us. Then coming from the left I sighted a troop of men running alongside in formation. They were pushing the steps that would reach the cockpit. No time for rituals now everything pulled out to meet the crisis at hand. With the last bit of energy left I over took the air steward and am running at the same speed as the plane. I gazed up to see the passengers peering down and waving. Suddenly the plane stops as though frozen in motion, the steps are attached and I am ushered up. It was a long way up those steps and with little time for conjuring up an explanation. So when I entered the plane to face the awaiting audience I put my hands to my head, then to my mouth at the same time as bowing profusely, and then I hid away in the nearest corner. I believe this culture is now catching on, and with endurance I am learning.

The other occasions of crisis and chaos occurred whilst working in Kushiro and Nagoya. In Kushiro I was due to appear at a small Cabaret on the edge of town. On my arrival I noticed that the dressing rooms were well equipped with everything at your fingertips to assist you in performance. The stage was huge with all the high tech equipment of lighting and sound. The reputation of these places went hand in hand with the quality of accommodation. It was good and luxurious. Direction was given to the shower, wash rooms and hot towels were left on the side. Refreshments were available at a single request and nothing was too much trouble. However five seconds before performance a small Japanese man came running into the dressing room muttering 'lackice, 'lackice', at the same time as bowing directly in front of me. I thought it was hardly the right time to be worrying me with such rituals and particularly to be anxiously bombarding me with such utterances I couldn't understand. In six inch stilettos heels, a grey silver llama dress and wrapped up in feather plumage I swooned past him with no intention of heeding to such nonsense. With great exuberance I made my entrance. Well at least I did one side of the stage. However before I knew it I was being exhumed by a cloud of smoke. Suddenly out of control I was now travelling at a rate of knots through a tunnel of mist. A little different to the elegance of entry I am now holding onto the plumage of feathers in the fear of life itself. My bottom hits the floor with a thud and my dress slid up to my waist as my bear flesh swam through a water drenched floor. With legs astride I slid the whole length of the stage by-passing the orchestra at an angle I had never experienced before. Dishevelled and in a state of shock I sat there for several seconds attempting to establish my whereabouts. I now looked like a half-plucked chicken ready for slaughter. The same man who had uttered those delayed words of wisdom was crouched and cowered before me as though awaiting his hour of doom. As I glanced at him in vengeance so he dropped to his knees in submission. Six attendants in flux and fury came hurriedly to the scene. They rummaged the stage for the aftermath of plumage and followed the trail to where another drama was about to take place. The warning of 'Black Ice' had been mistakenly ignored and at my own peril, and yet my hosts were there in good spirit, ready to manage the aftermath of affairs.

Another occasion when something like this had happened was in Nagoya. Cut into the centre of the stage floor was a circled platform that could be used for the purpose of elevation and decent. It descended to the basement and could ascend to six foot in the air. After some persuasion and reassurance that I wouldn't be propelled past ground level to the roof I agreed to try the apparatus out. On boarding the piece equipment I was already feeling sea sick and insecure. As it crept upwards I started panicking wondering whether to abandon flight. As the floor moved up pass ground floor level I moved backwards in hesitation and then on decent the trail of my costume jammed between the cracks where the two floor levels met. I was stuck. I couldn't move forward, backwards or sideways. I just froze with stage fright. And then with one almighty, unwomanly like tug

I not only split the costume full length but went catapulting five foot to the other side of the stage and landed alongside a stage prop of wilting blooms. A comic strip couldn't have been funnier. In all honestly I just felt lucky on having survived the flight in one piece. However, only to be asked by my hosts whether I could start again?

The friendships made during my travels were more valuable than the differences that separated us from them. We laughed, loved and bled the same and that was more important than any ceremonial or practised ritual. More important was the openness, the chance to share and authenticate relationship. This could be sometimes detected in a passing smile, the touch of a hand or a gesture of expressions. It was these single gestures that outweighed all. The only overt racist incident I experienced whilst in Japan was when walking with my Brazilian friend in a small village near to where we were working. Several children approached us chanting 'gaijin, gaijin', meaning foreigner. It wasn't long before the chants became aggressive and led to the throwing of stones. In fear we ran for our lives. However, it doesn't stop me empathising with those who take such offence at difference. In fact it alerted me to the fears, insecurities and suspicions that they must have experienced on seeing someone so unlike themselves. It prompts me to examine my own attitudes in the face of overwhelming insecurity. What are we doing identifying with the aggressor you might well ask? Well yes, if we don't do that we will always ignore the potential destructiveness lying deep in the crevices of our own shadows. It's from the point of our own understandings that we can begin to discover our differences, challenge our perception, and work towards change.

Being in the minority is an interesting experience. Working alone in some of the more remote areas of Japan accentuated a sense of isolation. It was an experience that brought with it empathy and depth of understanding for others dispossessed of culture and language. As much as you attempt and affiliate yourself with the custom of any one host Country you always remain to be different particularly the way in which you perceive and react. I do believe that we can learn from these unique differences. Differences that can inform and break down barriers. It's the essence of difference that can opportune a wider and wiser understanding and thus inspire our lives lived.

So you might ask, is being in the minority something to be aware of? I can only think that it is healthy to continue to punctuate and represent the minority in all its colour and splendour and continue to let it influence us in our relationships with one another. That's not to infer that the majority does not serve to have its own qualities. One does not have an advantage or disadvantage over the other. On the contrary as long as it serves to complement and teach; and raise awareness that it is the difference between the two that will cultivate and develop growth. Despite many differences in Japanese culture I have chosen to raise the nature of their caricature in moments of crisis and chaos as though it were an unforgivable weakness and yet in all fairness my stories describe an excellence and ease in the management of such incidents. Perhaps we all need to take time to examine our own weird and wonderful characteristics of culture; and have a good laugh at the quirks of reactions that affect us as nation on mass. Japanese culture alone is an example of how we might allow ourselves to be influenced and developed. The way in which it enthuses its workforce is original and compelling. The allegiance it builds and the spirit de core it nurtures and promotes is unique, and something to be envied.

My travels to Japan taught me much about myself and the prejudices that I had secured at heart. It was a refreshing experience and in reflection helped me move on from a hard place of rigid belief. There was something more precious than the harbouring of grudges. Something that challenged and melted all barriers and boundary. I believe it starts with acceptance, moves on through the storms of forgiveness to authenticate compassion and the ability to love. It's a life's journey that some of us will never encounter or begin. Did my experience of Japan touch my father's heart, release him in expression, and bring me closer in relationship. On my return we shared many stories about Japanese custom and culture. We laughed and joked about different caricatures in nature but nothing touched or inspired him to express the horrors of war. The hidden silences and truth's of his experience were buried and under lock and key. And so I was only left holding the healing of self in what might appear, as a repeated journey and phase, from one generation to the next.

Chapter 6

Holding the Environment

Della had been up all night holding on to the last thread of patience. The kids had barricaded themselves in a bedroom and there was no way of getting in. The bedroom window was wide open, music was blaring out into the night and miscellaneous items were being thrown out of the window. Della didn't remember what exactly started it all off other than the expectation of attending school the next day. Water flooded the kitchen and bathroom, streams of toilet paper decked the hall and the waste bins had been emptied out onto the floors. Della's colleague was covered in flour and standing there dripping wet. The whole place was full of energy like an electric current. Della and her colleague had run out of strategies and had exhausted all negotiation. This drama was now running into senseless entertainment and an obvious demonstration of power. Chaos now ruled and it wasn't going to be easy to eradicate the behaviour that had moved in. It was going to be a long sift, a question of time, wit and a battle over tiredness.

Both Della and her colleague sat down close to the barricaded door hoping to overhear the next intention. Thinking upon the behaviours locked in on themselves Della and her colleague attempted to work out the pecking order, the strongest to the weakest, from the most disturbed to the most audacious and bizarre. What behaviours would cancel themselves out in such a small space? Who would maintain leadership? How would allegiance be demonstrated? Who would show that allegiance and how far would each one be prepared to go for the sake of recognition and respect? One has to think on the level of street credibility here. 'Lord of the Flies' is the nearest descriptive analogy. That means riding the most daring of behaviours whatever brings the most horror and amusement. The stage had been set but who was directing the drama and pulling the strings so violently? Who was benefiting from this performance and who had the most to loose? More importantly how was Della and her colleague going to save face for all four youngsters and allow them an escape route from the situation they had locked themselves into? Della thought if they were to gain access to the group dynamic at least they could sabotage the content from within. Even if it were for just a few seconds it would allow them enough time to split and reframe the group. Something will have to give to move this play forward. Any strategic action taken will demand sensitivity and a unison that demonstrates flexibility with strong boundaries. Anything could be going on behind the bedroom door bullying, sexual exploitation or drugs might be apparent and being used against wills. The group competition might have become so great that daring feats are taking central precedence or due to the pressure of cohesion someone might be self-harming without constraint. All this will demand a rigorous assessment of risk.

After some discussion and knowing all the individuals involved both Della and her colleague decide to wait and monitor. At all costs they would encourage negotiation and detract from unacceptable behaviour without loosing sight of their agreed boundaries. Safety for self and others would remain paramount. Satisfied that all four youngsters were safe and nothing untoward was happening they set up camp not far from the locked door. Della and her colleague's ploy would be one of deflection. They decide to detract from the ongoing saga and set up a drama of their own. Hopefully this would create enough curiosity that it would attract and demand investigation. They agreed between their selves that they would leave their proposed audience enough safe space in which to maneaovuer and wander if they so wished. Above all they agreed that they would not over react to their spectator's disruption or response. So, to begin they got lost in their conversation with one another. Now, in full debate they began to laugh, joke and jest. Della's colleague begins to play his part so well she hardly recognises him. He produces a pack of playing cards and with two large tubes of smarties they commence playing three card brag. Every action is emphasised in such a way that they hardly recognise one another. In just a few minuets the voices coming from the bedroom suddenly cease. The only hearty laughter is coming from Della and her colleague as they become totally emerged in their game to win. The bedroom door opens and is left ajar. Two youngsters strain their necks to see what's going on. Would this tacit of deflection be enough to move the situation on or would it be sabotaged to gain back power. The door shuts opens again and then one of the youngsters comes out, passes by and then back into another bedroom. Undeterred by the youngster's appearance and with no intention of challenge Della and her colleague continue their game. Again the youngsters peer out from behind the bedroom door then one of them passes by again but this time very slowly as though waiting for a response. The two players acknowledge him politely and immediately return to their game. Then without warning another two of the youngsters venture from the bedroom to see what's going on. One of them tentatively enquires 'What are you doing aren't you going to send us back to our bedrooms', 'No' Della replied'. Gosh, Della thought we are actually talking but for how long? Was this to be a move of division or submission? How were they going to follow this act through? Were they just setting their selves up to be the target for yet more disruption? Della's mind went back to previous incidents whilst working in adolescence residential settings. Incidents of flame throwing with hair lacquer canisters, lighters, smashed windows, water bombs, fire alarms being set off, and youngsters attempting to climb onto roofs. Della thought upon the times they had talked youngsters down from high ledges, trees, bridges and school roofs. Is it just coincidence that youngsters climb up towards higher pinnacles when acting out thought Della or is it a natural demand coming from an emotional state of being. Is there a sense of omnipotence up there, or is it that there is no where else to go?

Working in residential units for adolescence can be a challenging experience and being prepared and proactive in the face of such disturbances is sometimes the only line of defence. The ability to sense atmosphere, anticipate action and foresight of events can be a useful survival kit. In such situations limiting and closing down space is essential with the kitchen being the first and most dangerous area. Della knew whatever the riot might involve the only valuable tools that workers had were the relationships established with the youngsters. As frail as the relationships might be in such scenario's they were a vital lifeline never to be underestimated. Della recalls one incidence when she was on the wrong side of a door with youngsters crowding her into a corner. Just before pursuing their revenge one of the youngsters stood between Della and her attackers demanding that they stop. Della knew them all individually and knew her rescuer well. However, she never thought that this character was capable of showing an ounce of mercy whatever occasion. Della could not think of any reason for such an action except the time invested in listening to the grief of family affairs and accepting him unconditionally. It was times like these that you suddenly realise who your real allies are. She remembers this episode as having changed her view and approach towards all such troubled youngsters and similar actions of riot. It had given her an extra faith in human nature and the understanding that whatever the chaos caused, as long as no one was in danger, then that was ok. It's the acceptance of being out of control in situations of riot that often calms the storm. She recalled yet another incident in which a youngster was presenting bizarre behaviour so much so that the peer group had learnt to ignore him whenever possible. In the beginning it had been a fun band wagon for all the youngsters however over time they had got tired of his performances. It would regularly commence at ten o clock when there was a change in shift. He would commence standing on his head, running around in circles and refusing to go to bed. He would slide down the stairs on a silver tray repeatedly and then start to open and close all widows and doors. He sang at the top of his voice at the same time as jumping from one piece of furniture to the next. It was a complex set of behaviours that one could never anticipate, and was acted out in solitude and persistence. To see how far he would go Della and her colleague decided to work alongside his drama. In response he ushered them into a room and loosely tied Della's colleague up with a rope. He then dressed up in a discarded workman's overall. Leaving the front door wide open he took a step ladder out into the front garden, climbed to the top and using a piece of wood for a baton he started conducting an imaginary orchestra, at the same time as singing at the top of his voice. It was difficult to decide how aware he was of his behaviour and how this was effecting others. What was important was his need of Della and her colleague being part of the audience. His behaviour demanded them to be available at all costs. However, when Della locked the door in order to free up her colleague he became irritated and frantic in his efforts to gain access. His face swelled up in rage and tears began to flow. The fear of exclusion and being locked out became evident. It was from this that Della and her colleague were able to push forward in addressing some of the underlying angst's, fears as well as the overlapping repertoire of behaviours presented.

Della thoughts suddenly returned to the present saga. They were now faced with all four youngsters viewing the charade being played. Della dared not give their presence a flinch of her attention in fear of giving the game away. Her colleague is now acting out his glee after winning most of the smarties. In fact he is now so lost in role Della begins to wonder who needs rescuing. The drama is so intense that they have attracted the attention of all the youngsters. Two of them attempt to give Della assistance in selecting her cards. However, Della is not going to listen to any suggestion at this stage. After all the audience consists of outsiders who have not yet genuinely joined the game. In response one of them grabs two smarties and swallows them. Della's colleague ignores the action reimburses Della with two more and the game is off again. Della's colleague's pockets are now full of smarties. He rubs his hands as though in victory and begins to tuck into his guarded winnings. Della has ten smarties left and three aces in hand. Della's state of loss suddenly attracts three advisers. Della attempts to cut her losses and surrender but her followers are insistent on holding ground. However there is just one youngster missing from the scene. In good faith Della hands her cards over to her supporters whilst she goes to seek the missing person. She eventually finds him in his bedroom staring at all the pictures of his family lined up on a shelf. Unable to express himself he pushes her out of the room and shuts the door. It's not the time for enquiry. He will need his private space to weep away his sadness. She waits outside the door and assures him that she is there and can listen if he permits. She attempts to humour him but gets no response. Perhaps this was the source from which the affray commenced. However, that would be hard to determine being that each one had as equal a sad story to tell.

With the group dynamic now calm and dissolved, tiredness began to seep in for all the partakers. Della and her colleague took advantage of the situation and began to usher the youngsters to bed, but not without first sharing the winnings. How would they begin to address the behaviour acted out? Well nothing would be addressed until tomorrow. Tomorrow was another day and would come soon enough. Della looked at her colleagues with glee and then retorted, 'Don't ever gamble in front of the children, unless you are always willing to loose the game or the parts played'. Youngsters are only too aware of how to work their Carers, where their weaknesses lie.

Youngsters have an antenna that is sharp and sensitive and their accustomed behaviours will bend according to the sets and pairs of staff as well as to the approach given to hold that environment. Youngsters need to know that you can accept and understand the ugly and demonstrative sides of their selves and will more often than not provoke rejection as a way of testing your ability to hold the environment. Adam Phillips(1988 p.89) refers to Winnicott quotes,

'…..If he is not hated, if what is unacceptable about him is not acknowledged then his lovableness and love will not feel fully real to him'.

The conditions of environment are invaluable as it can open up a sphere of possibilities. We ourselves can be used as containers of expression. Being open to such expression can be the ultimate challenge to the unknown parts of self. However, it's only in our abilities to accept our own shadows and acknowledge our own limitations and fallibility that will ultimately encourage honesty, openness and spontaneity. In response instead of being the figures of control we suddenly become human and loving holders of others and their environments. Thorne (2002 p79) quotes,

'To be 'alive' 'alive' is to risk being fully present to another in the conviction that we can trust the core of our own being.

It's ok to get things wrong. It's ok not to be ok. In the light of such conditions one is able to cultivate trusting relationships and promote potential. With the stage now set anything can happen within. It's the quality of holding environment and the content within that will surely tell its tale.

St. Matthew Chapter 19 verse 14
'But Jesus said, Suffer little children, and forbid them not to come unto me for of such is the Kingdom of heaven'.

Chapter 7

In Sacrifice to Managements
The Ilusion And Disolusionment Of Change

The building is a huge iron casket purposely built against unwelcome invasion. Its awesome presence stands in the middle of a rundown estate on the edge of town. This building is a central piece of machinery that adds insult to those that live in its Community. Ivy grows up all sides of the building covering and disguising its fortitude. Surveillance is evident from all corners of the building and secures all entrances to and from. The inside décor and environment is arranged to create a sense of space. The subtle colours of mauve and pinks soothe and calm the cutting edge of the dual purpose to protect and reign. This new Local Authority building already has a history of unrest. There have been incidents that have taken place here and the perpetrators never found. Internal politics are guarded so well that abuses are hidden from view. This has become a part of the culture and understanding. It's similar to a system under siege with its ethos built upon the power to control. Sanitising the contents of labour in this building has brought a new set of people here to work. However a sense of suspicion and insecurity holds fast to a history of unresolved conflict. It's a house divided against itself with the ghosts of the past ruling with a vengeance for justice. Tyranny breeds tyranny and without doubt feeds into the climate and culture of environment and community. Its going to take guts, nerve and being in touch at all levels for this organisation to change the status quo. The defensive mode adopted by the people it serves is only too understandable. They have few weapons and often result to an animal instinct of fight or flight. The culture of 'us and them' is a feature that has become rigid in its nature. The walls are so thick between that the calls of surrender are barely heard. Its do or die.

For Emma moving from a familiar and facilitative work environment to the unknown feels exciting but scary. Being at the heart of new beginnings for the purpose of changing what has gone before is an opportunity in itself. The challenge would consist of building a new sense of justice for the people Emma served. It will involve the breaking down of barriers between us, them and others. New open and honest relationships will be the foundations for a new sense of Community with families at the heart of their own lives, decisions and choice. It will be their vision that will keep all of us focused.

Two years into the work and the teams are up and running and working towards full capacity. Members of the teams represent a whole range of cultural and ethnical backgrounds and all have varying degrees of skill and expertise. As the work becomes more stimulating so the workers become more engrossed with their noses hard to the grind. Pressure builds up alongside time schedules and it not long before the symptoms of strain begin to show. Subsequently pockets of family dynamic bursts froth into the play of team life. Threatened with the loss of control the lead player panics and begins to strut up and down like a cock pacing out its dilemma. The mask of humour no longer holds but instead there is a stench of poisoned wit. A slant of verbal expression now sets precedence and in return erodes principle, value and desecrates the vision once held. A mentality under siege now comes to the fore. In defence it weaves itself through a battalion of forged relationships, taking refuge in any given social allegiance. It's a bitter sweet soul threatened by its own inebriated survival.

The leader masquerades his power throughout the department and without consultation begins to organise his barracks of defence. No longer able to cope with the complexities of a diversified approach he begins to yield an autocratic rule over everything. Suspicion and fear takes its course and seeps into the once established and trusted relationships Negotiation is difficult and the sense of solidarity towards change is lost. Team members take up their guard as they bow down to the new and unexpected order. Whispers of discontent emerge but no one has the courage of energy to challenge. One member aligns herself with a culture of vilification; another member offers himself up as scapegoat, whilst two others split off and lie low. Unable to hide from this dynamic of cohesion Emma takes up a reckless stance against the barbarous lead however only to bring herself into the full view his repute. It was only weeks before she crawled towards the exist as a way of escape, dragging with her a system of battered beliefs. Balled out in one strike! On departure she senses the doors closing in completion of an episode of time in delusion. The bolts and locks ricochet into place as she passes through. Looking back is painful and much loss is felt in its place. In pressing forward she can hear the echoes of the doors closing tight upon the past.

Opening the doors again was a long and arduous journey. The locks to the doors were fastened hard and it was more than her strength alone that will unlock them. But it was not just one door there were many.

Moving On

Leaving her professional position proved to be a huge loss. Stress combined with sickness had taken its toll and she was unable to keep pace. The battle in the years of recovery was a painful experience with the loss of confidence being a continual struggle. During these years Emma joined an employment agency and endeavoured to keep herself financially buoyant. There was no guarantee of work and no income if you fell sick. Her future appeared bleak. In fact it was a period in which she gave up a future to live instead a day at a time. During this period she was fortunate to have worked for many different organisations both statutory and voluntary. It was probably the most humbling of experiences in her life. It felt like peddling a bike backward through time with a head-full of knowledge and skills that had been put on hold. She had to remind herself that she was now an Agency worker an outsider; an affordable and dispensable commodity; a cog in the wheel unaffected by a rank of allegiance and with little power to effect change.

Within this time she experienced some of the most professional to the crudest of management's. Some of the systems were ridden by archaic and rigid power structures. This was sometimes due to a lack of professionalism, training, knowledge and supervision but some of it was just pure ignorance to the needs of others. It was Care given at its crudest. The only stance one can take here is by keeping your values at heart and continually acting them out hoping it will cause contagion. The worst scenarios she recalls were in the Care for the Elderly.

For Emma it took no time to determine the dynamic approach and politic of any one team. However, joining groups and teams was probably the most time consuming and enduring task of all. It sometimes took a struggle and fight to nudge your way in. Ripples of insecurity and suspicion would rickashade throughout its organism. Joining might be compared to a battle of survival, and then only to exit at the end of just another contract. The sole advantage was that of earning a living from a distance. What safer place could one possess? Let me give you an instance of Emmas experience as she tells it verbatim.

'You've done it again. A quick encounter with group dynamics, before rushing to the surface for air. In all good faith and honesty I joined up yesterday. I had accepted a contract working for a reputable mental health organisation. I would be employed to work in various Communities city wide. I jumped at the opportunity. I had a sincere interest in the aspects of mental health and held great empathy for those who suffered as a result of enduring mental health difficulties. With a Girl Guide purpose at heart I was ready to bulldoze myself into everybody's life and need. Armed with various tools for shaping and influencing I instantly presented myself as a picture of skill and confidence. My tools were sharp and cut deep, leaving no room for rough edges. My aim and vision is for a subject of fitting; systematically packed and ready for purchase. An Angel of perfection; my very own work of art.

Equipped with self-awareness I had already become aware of my over zealous nature to get on with the job. With much irritation I endeavoured to suppress the angst of excitement felt. Wake up dreamer! You remember something about reality don't you? Equipped with a good sense of cause and humour I begin to laugh at the achievable chunks of life scattered along the roadside. Incisions into the pieces of pain left hanging on lampposts during the journey home. But wait who was that hanging there. Wrenching my neck without looking too close that it might contagiously infect I suddenly realise it's a piece of me. In fourth gear and with haste I avoid a third glance and let it hang there in the remnants of memory. Might I go back on further inspection'?

The contract of work offered engaged Emma with a complementary team who possessed much skill, knowledge and experience in its own field. However, her encounter lasted just three weeks enough time to assess the dynamic of personalities and group cohesion. The team's unguarded performance was that of a universal trance and dance acted out for a leaders suffocating approval and gratification. It was a brief punishing and placating experience. The dance was tightly held together at all costs by what appeared to be an insecure and persecutory self. Verbal innuendoes made by its leader were indirectly targeted at different individuals who were then left in a quandary as to the extent of their poe far. Much later on and in the light of truth they would be approached, picked up, dusted off and then given a peck up talk. What an act, what a reproach thought Emma.

Colleagues had learnt to sit in their glee being that it was not their turn. Although Emma could not deny a deep empathy for the accused and the period of disapproval experienced. The walk to the executioner's yard was enduring. Rescuing was prohibited and would only bring you into the limelight to take yet another turn of reproof. The clutching power of reprieve was heavily guarded and solely owned by an executioner's hand. However, with all this in mind it was very much on to the next meeting in which a replicated pattern of behaviour would occur. Again un-coded messages of projection would seep out from the barrage of verbal content and suddenly pin you up against the wall. Oh dear that's me, and again!

Life in a Box

Here we go again. Emma has left one work environment to join another. She has been placed with two colleagues who have been thrust together with a triad of others, one of whom will ultimately take the lead. Two of them have a distant relationship compared to the three. The others have well established relationships which go beyond professional boundaries. There is a natural reluctance at the stage of joining and a sense of insecurity felt on either side. The force of group dynamics fills the centre stage and begs them all to fall into a natural pecking order. There is a push and pull of emotion as individuals fight for position. With much reluctance Emma resists, in a hope to build in a new dynamic that might free up human expectation and the space in which to work. This ruffles the feathers of defensive and internal players who strive for Emma to take up the regulation of order. However, the attempts to nudge Emma into position fail miserably. Unfortunately, irritated players leave Emma no option other than to over enact the role of scapegoat, an unlovable position but a vital role of catharsis. The colleague who Emma has moved over with runs the expected course in a bid to find a favourable position within the three. However, all favourable positions are occupied and it's not long before she tires of the fight, surrenders and leaves. The triadic formation of relationship they now have yields to a powerful expectation of ranking. Ranking is based upon time invested in personal relationships rather than on a collective unit of professionalism and wisdom. The leader's natural attraction towards followers is evident. Followers or internal leaders must be able to give emotional support, personal affirmation and be faithful enough to cover all fallibility. A follower can be detected at a distance and is ultimately adorned with grace and favour. The dance for support takes on a regular pattern and in response a reciprocal dance of parroting and mimicry follows.

Leadership played from the position of personality. It's interesting how it draws upon its defences at the same time as checking it's doubled sided back. At ease it weaves itself in and out with as many masks as there are players. Priming each and every feather it picks and pecks at anything or anyone who is audacious enough to be out of step. It demands reassurance and searches out all approval and applause. It's not good to be working to your ability rather its better to keep any potential hidden from view, in case of ridicule. What becomes more apparent is the culture of hidden messages played out in language, action and deed. If you're not part of it then you will forever remain outside its secure perimeters. One learns to walk on egg shells in order that the centre holds with itself. It's so tempting to nudge it at the core, to stamp on the hardness of its shell and release the pocket of life within. What sabotage you may think but what a relief. It produces opportunities of change and breath breathed for the first time. However running up stream for the sake of change or no change is a tiring effort. So instead they all guard the drama with their lives bend to its nature, at the same time as stifling their own growth, development and potential. In tune to the saga Emma wriggles like a worm under a naked flame. She steps backwards, forwards and then ends up crawling sideways like a crab to escape the inside of an empty box

And in Conclusion

If we accept and become complacent in our own illusions it can be a difficult place from which to move on from. So it's with this in mind Emma presses on in hope. And so Emma continues to be part of many groups, to experience its organism and cycles. She dances the dance, affiliates with its ethos and is able to accustom herself to rule and regulation. She now does this with little effort or strife and has learnt to keep moving on with a sense of enquiry at heart. Flexibility, love and patience cannot be ruled out in this process. The biggest challenge has been living at the heart of her own vulnerabilities and fallible nature as well as the learning gained from forgiveness and humility through the process of group affairs. It's sometimes a portrayal of weakness that serves to open others to the beginning of an authentic relationship. With grace she continues to learn.

Other lessons learnt in the process of group life have been the acceptance of dynamic and role played. The dynamic of anyone group is often influenced by roles played. This is where the dance begins. Balanced to this is the variety of those roles. A role, be it catalyst, goat or clown are all essential and if recognised for what they are can be 'played out' to benefit the group particularly in the awareness and effort of breaking down barriers that separate and divide. Again, the acceptance of difference and the value of its potential have much more to teach. And so Emma continues to learn from all her experiences of group life, its processes and gives much time to the values at stake in the vision held and the potential for change.

What do you suppose it's like up there in the management of heavens affairs? Do you suppose that Gods management is full of wrath as it rules and reigns? Is he a ruthless God in his dealings ready to oppress and subjugate in call to the power he yields. Will the breath from his nostril burn up all those who dare to dissent. In heavens side stage drama might we witness Zeus in his power struggle over Poseidon? Will the thunder of discontent cause Hades to burst forth in a bid to reign? How might God respond? Would he look on in his ease and cause the heavens to grate against the earth in a demand for allegiance. Would the ocean bow its waves in obedience to his omnipotence? Would he be forced to spit out its coals of fire? What do you suppose Gods management style emulates? Is he an inclusive presence of awesomeness, an enabler perhaps, or facilitator; a teacher in all the aspects of truth, humility and justice? In thought Emma wonders about the Plaines of heaven and the power that rules. On arrival will we all be caught up in an awesome battle for justice or will we forever wander through the ages of time in contentment? Will there be a scrabble for position in some heavenly form of bid and bow. Will it be a case of 'who you are?' or more apparent, 'who you know?' Or will God be all forgiving, one who accepts unconditionally, and values everything Emma is and has to offer? If that's so will Emma's transcendent body pass through another with ease and without discord, or will she just be an archetype stuck between enemy and foe without wings. With a thousand thoughts in mind Emma is already on my knees in forgiveness and in request praying for a fitting place where she might rest or more appropriately a place where she might fit. Or might this also be an illusion awaiting change?

Chapter 8

Her name was Irene

Her name was Irene. She was a medium sized, stout woman of fifty eight with a fresh complexion. One side of her nose constantly ran with mucus. On prompting she would hurriedly and apologetically produce several broken pieces of tissue in an attempt to halt its flow. Her hair was parted in the middle and was draped down either side of her face. It was a two tone colour of red, with grey roots. Despite the hair being well groomed at the front the back was so badly matted that it hung on the back of her head like a thatched shelf. It was going to be difficult to convince her to have this cut out. It was heavy and must have felt part of her over the years. Irene had an awkward gate and often stood nursing her arthritic arm. Shuffling to and fro in response to medication she had little sense of personal distance and would often stand so close that one was forced to back or side step. Interaction was like an awkward waltz danced out in an untimely step. Her clothing was grubby, unmatched and gave little shape or elegance. Her skirts were far too short and would hitch up between her buttocks as she walked. Ill chosen tops revealed her breasts and the rhythm of her movement. Her walk was distinct. She would waddle with her feet turned in as though in pain. On further inspection of her feet Mary detects that Irene's toe nails are so overgrown that they were growing sideways and crippling her every step. Similar were her finger nails that had begun to curve over, obstructing her grip. It was as though she had no sense of her outer shell or its barnacles. She was content enough to accept and work with whatever the growth or pain experienced. There was no apparent connection with self-care or the ease that it might have brought. She was just Irene. She was a simple character with an innocent childlike nature. Her eyes were bright, full of curiosity and fun, always ready to connect with someone who might give her the time of day. Irene was of a compliant nature and chose to ignore anything that might challenge. She would often burst forth in frivolous conversation and then guardedly await a response. If information was complex she would end up repeating the last two syllables as a way of saying that she had heard. Her agreances were persistent but her intention was often the opposite. Whilst working alongside Irene, Mary quickly learnt to address and re-address everything they agreed upon in an effort to gain genuine choice or opinion.

Irene had recently moved into a one bedroom flat. The accommodation was in disarray. A chinchilla occupied the corner to the living room. There were a swarm of flies about the place and a strong sweet stench in the air. It was going to take some time to build up a trusting relationship with Irene. Irene didn't come alone. Placed in the corner of the bedroom she had possessions amounting to twenty five black dustbin liners full of items that she guarded with her life. How was she going to trust Mary with what had become an extenuation of self. Marys head spun with curiosity. What had she been collecting that had been so precious? Where would she begin? Irene looked at Mary and grinned as though in response and then said, 'I had to get rid of the dogs.

Irene had a male friend who she had previously lived with and of whom she was very fond. They had been together for a number of years and only separated on occasions when Irene possessions took precedence and space became limited. These occasions forced Irene into searching abodes elsewhere. Wherever Irene ventured the baggage would follow, baggage that guaranteed her security and existence. It appeared to be a repeated pattern. On each separation from her partner she would be forced to shed yet another load of baggage before returning to live with him. It was hard to assess their relationship as Mary had never met him or seen them together. Irene told Mary on several occasions that he was dreaming of one day winning the lottery so that he could buy a self contained property in Conrnwall. However, Mary never heard once that the dream included Irene. On questioning her about his dream and the part she would play she just giggled and then replied, 'he might ask me to go with him, might he?' Mary suddenly felt like a mother tackling an unsure answer. In response Mary just looked at her and smiled.

In commencing work alongside her Mary gave little attention to the accumulated possessions and instead concentrated on her health, how she felt and how she was managing the distance that separated her from her partner. At first she was a little bemused and guarded by Mary's involvement but it wasn't long before her defences dropped and she became more relaxed. Together they attended her immediate surroundings, ridding the accommodation of flies and putting some sense of order about the place. It was a long haul but an essential task if they were to tackle anything beneath the surface, whether it was material, flesh or emotion. They sometimes worked very hard. At times she would stop me to ask when Mary was coming next. Mary always took this as a sign that she had done enough, so they would stop and plan for the next visit.

Irene and Mary got to know one another well over the weeks and months of working together. She told Mary much about her life, past relationships and the experience of family life. On sharing information of Mary's hometown Bristol Irene immediately interrupted and said, 'I can't go back ther, I'm too frightened'. Irene told Mary a vivid account of her experience. As though it was yesterday she described an event of being kidnapped. Intrigued by the detail and content Mary urged her on to tell her more. During a night out at the Holiday Inn

Irene had been accosted by a number of men. They had taken her away in a van and placed her in a dungeon beneath the ground. She was absolutely convinced that they were travellers because they weren't in uniform. She thought that she had spent a number of days in capture but was unsure. With eyes full of fear she could hardly describe her overwhelming angst. Irene's expression alone told Mary of her plight. In continuing her story the irises of her eyes slid to the corner of their openings as if the evil were still lingering in the shadows. It was awaiting her destiny that had been so debilitating. Irene did not know what they had planned or what they were going to do to her. With little control or power over her situation she became fretful and distraught almost as though she were reliving her experience. Mary done her best to empathise with her arrest and calm the menacing memory. Encouraged by Marys response Irene then added, 'the next thing I knew they had put me back in the van, they put a mask over my face and when I awoke I was in hospital. I haven't been back to Bristol since.' In all innocence of listening Mary was at least relieved to hear the outcome of her tale. 'Someone must have rescued you then,' Mary replied. 'Yeh, Irene said, but I don't' want to go back ther again'. Mary never challenged Irene's story or suggested that Irene might have been unwell at the time as it was too early into the relationship and there were too many other pressing issues.

Both Mary and Irene had begun sorting out the bin liners that were fall to the brim. Irene appeared content and secure in knowledge that her possessions were to be handled with sensitivity and care. Subsequently, she began to eagerly await Mary's visits. Over the weeks to follow it became a project in itself, but a satisfying one as Mary began to notice Irene become more at ease and content in herself, as though she had unleashed a burden. They divided the possessions into three piles of what she wanted to keep, throw away or donate to Charity. Many of the items had their own story to tell. Bundles of clothing now obviously to small revealed Irene's past anguished struggle with anorexia. It was a sad story told of loosing the will to eat and the eventuality of hospital admission. Other items portrayed a life style of glamour beauty and fashion. Amongst a bundle of soft cuddly toys was a large number of Cindy Dolls including a giant sized model of Ken's Car. Irene clutched on to them as though she knew everyone. Together they filled another three bags with make up and Jewellery. All the cosmetic's and jewellery were still in the bags when originally bought along with their price tags. There were enough goods to open a small shop. Watching Irene open the packages was like watching a child at Christmas eager, with excitement and always surprised by the contents. Amongst the goods was the odd box of out of date biscuits and chocolates still in tact and in its original cellophane covering. The out of date boxes marked some of Irene's load as being more than seven years old. Mary wondered sadly why she had not been helped with this before. Had medication become more important than the input of time and compassion? Irene's load revealed much about the way she saw her world. The number of Cindy dolls and amount of make up and jewellery revealed the images of desire that were perhaps lodged in mind. How did she see herself? Were the dolls a replacement for self? If that were the case the images of self and her ideal world were far apart from the reality lived.

Mary got to know Irene very well over the weeks. She shared with her the separation and loss of past relationships, the loss of parents and the loss of a son to adoption in the face of tragic circumstances of health. Despite her fates Irene was full of life. She reminded Mary of a cork in the ocean battered by the waves and yet so buoyant. Irene's wishes for another child took Mary by surprise. Mary was speechless, but when catching Irene' eye she detected such a passion to love, her instant judgements vanished. If anyone could give love it was surely Irene. Being so unlovely and unloved herself and touched by such losses in life, she had more to give than any. Robbed by her mental and physical health she was at the mercy of her own vulnerabilities. Living at the heart of those vulnerabilities gave her the permission to teach others the love she had to share. Much of her love had been poured out on the animals she had owned. Sadly due to irregular management she had lost the animals one by one. Irene talked about them with much affection. She could trust her animals more than humans; they were dependable and never cut the air with their vicious tongues. The yearning for companionship, love and the need to give love in return was so evident and at the heart of Irene's needs.

Did the quality of time given have any long term effect upon Irene, her beliefs, outlooks and behaviour? Last time Mary saw her she was wearing a distinctive hat similar to her own. Matching was a scarf wrapped around her in a familiar style to Marys own. The matted mass of hair had been cut out which had taken ten years off of her appearance. Mary had not yet managed to talk her into a small operation that would have rectified the constant flow of mucus or the operation needed on her hand to maximise movement. Irene insisted that she didn't want to waste time in a hospital, not even for a day. Too many sad days and moods linger in the familiar walls and corridors of hospital wards. However, with little prompting she had begun cutting her finger nails; her toe nails had been cut and she was walking with ease. She had agreed to regular visits from cleaners who would help her with caring for the Chinchilla and the organisation of her flat. Mary wondered whether in years to come that someone would continue to give her the quality of time she needed. Would they care enough to remind her of her appearance and give her the encouragement and reward of time in relationship or might we find in years to come that Irene is stuck within the ever revolving doors of an institution.

Today's Systems and institutions are ridden with proto-call, checklists and procedures that it sometimes serves to exclude rather than include. The exclusion of not belonging or fitting into an appropriate category is the ultimate fear and fate. The culture of institutions appears to have swept us along in a tide of efficiency. The quick fix of medication has preference over allotted time and compassion. That's not to say that the quick fix doesn't work or is not essential but Mary is sceptical of its long term effect. The system of being pre-packed and processed like a chain of fast food store comes to mind. Time saving methods and efficiency appears to be the order of the day however Mary remains sceptical of its play on statistics and whether it truly only lends itself to industry and the next ballot box. Working with ever increasing workloads, expectations and pressures of performance we have probably forgotten about the advantages of affording genuine time to one another and those with whom we work and serve. Instead we have become sad strangers in our own homes, communities and workplaces.

Chapter 9

Beyond Addiction

As soon as Ella arrives Tony releases a barrage of unconnected statements.

'I've forgotten the day and time can you remind me? I haven't slept for years at least it feels that way. I've been walking up and down the sitting room trying to get out the door for hours but haven't quite managed it. I've been thinking about the incident of assault on the neighbour and the injustice of it having been taken to Court. If I haven't been put through enough? Loosing the residence of my own flat for six months and then to be tagged. There's noises coming from the tag I'm wearing and I think I am being watched. Look at that red light on the television I've never noticed that on before and it goes off every time I move. Do you think the neighbours can see me? I am so anxious that I am unable to take my clothes off to bathe; I have to check all the rooms before proceeding. My mind tells me that they are out to kill me. Do you think they are? I think they are seeping up through the floorboards especially that witch who accused me of the assault. Do you think she can get to me with her witchcraft? She is going to kill me I know because I saw a man in the car with a bug. Every time I listen I can hear them as though they are in the room. I'm not a well man, why do they want to hurt me. Don't they think that I have suffered enough? Can you hear them laughing at me, listen! I know that perhaps that's the noise coming from the traffic outside but I'm not sure.'

On arrival at the home Ella finds Tony sat in the same room unshaven and dishevelled. He has his arm bandaged and he's lost weight. The living environment is more chaotic than normal with various items piled upon the living room coffee table. He appears over suspicious and paranoid. Nick tells Ella that he cut his arm in the bathroom and had to go to hospital for stitches. He then goes on to tell her about having to call an ambulance in an emergency because of turning yellow. In a very irritated manner Nick tells her how the ambulance men arrived on the scene looked around the door and disappeared without addressing his dilemma. Ella listens to him with much empathy. In response they talked through the belief of changing colour, how that was affecting him and in reality whether this was an emergency. Nick shrugs his shoulders as though to recount his thoughts, realised that in actual fact without tests, he could do nothing even if he were changing colour. After checking Ella's eye contact he then proceeds to tell her about the presence of his neighbours in the same room.' It's very strong and evident,' he says. As he describes the evil presence his frightened eyes search to the left and then to the right. Whilst listening Ella attempts to move the coffee table aside to make sense of the disorder however Nick becomes fearful and asks her if she can see the forces coming up from the floor. After assuring and reassuring him that there was nothing there Ella decides to sit down and just listen to him the best she can. Much of his illusion and fear was being triggered from the natural noises of the environment and the ozone's that rise as result of change in the atmosphere. However, as soon as they unravel and make sense of one illusion they are already at the beginning of another. During the following conversation Ella attempts to deflect from the dysfunctional thoughts to remind him of who he is, his past achievements, his wishes for the future and his ability to change the way things are however it feels like a loosing battle against imploding anxieties. These constant revels of thought are not even giving Nick a chance for rest. He can't remember when he last slept or ate and he is unable to think about going out. For a moment Ella doesn't know where to start. It is evident that his torment is relentless. Ella tentatively asks him whether he thinks a psychiatric assessment might be helpful however Nick is reluctant to agree to any sort of assessment that might deem him 'mentally insane'.

Nick is just thirty five years of age. He is in poor health and experiences emotional/mental health and addiction problems. His needs do not comfortably fit into the criteria of any one Service and as a result in the past he has been pushed from one agency to another. Such responses have only mirrored and perpetuated the fragmented existence he already experiences. It has not been easy to assess this case as well as identify and apply an effective and comprehensive approach that might promote independence and well being. Nick is a conscientious character who lacks self-confidence and esteem. His sense of powerlessness is crippling. Although he is very able to defend himself physically he sees himself as a victim. Nick is a very depressed and lonely individual. The problem he experiences from day to day accentuates the isolation he already feels. Nick lives from one self-induced psychosis to the next. His addiction to amphetamine is so severe that one might question as to whether he is in voluntary control. The quantity of substance used is massive and only serves to propel him into a world of paranoia and fear. The perpetual use of needles is just another means of ritualised self-abuse. It's a repeated cycle, not to feel real, but to push himself into a chaotic sense of non-being. This dual faced addiction appears to have created a will of its own and there seems no escape from its relentless demands. Nick has just become an exhausted slave and victim to the power of its cycle. He wants to be all that the substance offers and has handed himself over to its fate. It's left him with no true sense of self and he is unable to see himself without the affliction that is robbing him of his sanity. The symptoms have become the guarantee of a very tormented and sick existence. Symptoms of agoraphobia and severe panic attacks exacerbate Nick's mobility and day to day routines. Rather than venture out Nick will often choose to stay in his flat for days at a time. On some occasions he will get ready to go out but then it takes him up from four to six hours to pass through the front door. It sometimes takes a crisis to venture out.

The environment in which he lives is in a disordered state and drug paraphernalia litter the surfaces. Ella can detect Nick's mental state just by observing his habitat. Ella is presently concerned, as he is unable to concentrate to clear just one area of the floor. His delusions are running into one another and he is unable to give himself time to unveil and piece together his thoughts. It has been difficult to connect with him at any constructive level due to a self-induced psychosis. A state that has become the central organising theme of his life. When Ella arrives on visits he tends to pre-pack her into the momentum of his daily needs without giving any thought to change. Her refusal to fit in with his demands is frustrating but tolerated. This resistance is the only positive link with which she works.

Compounding Nick's complex needs is a saga of events that have occurred over the past nine months. It began with new neighbours moving into the flat beneath. Nick had been elated to think that he had made new friends of the same age. The only unfortunate factor was that they shared some of the same problems of addiction. It wasn't long before the friendship ran into problems and as a result there were several altercations with one of them landing Nick before the courts. Subsequently, Nick was charged with assault and was later tagged, fined, given an anti social behaviour order, and fifteen months supervision order. Since these events Nick has been obsessed with feeling of guilt and shame. He has tormented himself over the injustice of these events and has found it very difficult to move on in his resolution.

At the time of being charged, bail conditions meant that he had to move out of his own abode to reside with his mother. The spate of time awaiting sentence was seven months. It proved to be a very difficult time for Nick as he held a fractious relationship with his mother. The relationship he has with his mother is characterised by all the traits of co-dependency. Her solution to Nick's problem is one of control. She cannot see herself as being in a co-dependency relationship with her son and finds it very difficult to action any advice given. Instead she involves all agencies in her angst, and attempts to organise their powers of restraint over him. She never ceases her constant vigil over his personal affairs. This includes checking with Ella at times when Nick has rejected her. Nick sometimes interprets this as an evil plot to get rid of him and at times feels that his mother will not be satisfied until he is dead. He often feels suffocated and is fearful of her invasive intrusions. Nick is blind to his true self in the relationship he has with his mother. He hates and loves her. He yearns to be looked after by her and can't resist her persistent nurture; however when he is in dispute with her he despises her. This is a relationship in bondage and robbed of any true spiritual authenticity. Working alongside the relationship has had its problems. Although both mum and Nick have distinct and separate needs it is not difficult to get enmeshed and caught up between the two. There have been many times when they have attempted to sabotage one another and then vent this through Ella as third party. In the past, Nick has taken umbrage at Ella's concerns over his mother's welfare. Like a child with his own toy he has voiced his possession over the support being given. It's as though Nick wants to possess whatever belongs to him. He is desperate for someone to listen, believe and perceive his story with out reservation. Anything less is a betrayal. Although Ella is careful to hold onto the role of supporting Nick, it is necessary to continually adjust, balance and sometimes withdraw the time given. Nick has to accept that support isn't just an easy option of meeting needs and making things alright, it also consists of challenge, change and progress.

Nicks circumstances are for the present fixated, and awaiting a crisis to intervene. He is locked into a negative cycle of being. The sad affair about this case is that Nick is living within his own prison. He has created a false sense of self and reality and repeats the same failure to feel real, time and time again. He is lost to self and is unable to find the will or control over his life. He is presently an empty shell void of the authenticity of spirit. One might conclude that Nick is totally self indulged and acting out the role of a spoilt child. You might well ask why he is giving himself such a hard time. Why can he not just stop taking drugs for enough time to gain a strand of sanity? However it's not as easy as that. Addiction has been the only dependable and reliable relationship ever formed in Nick's life. The troubled years of childhood is characterised by abuse and rejection. There have been times when as a child he has not known who to turn to with the turmoil of emotions experienced. When the violent relationship of his parents ended he was used as an emotional battleground. Much anger was vented through Nick as he was pushed backwards and forwards between the two. Subsequently, as a child he lacked confidence worth and a good concept of self. He remembers a very sad existence at home and school.

Nick has chosen to freeze emotion out by the use of substances. Addiction is a viable solution for him. It gives purpose and reason for living and provides a culture, an identity and a sense of grouping with others. It's a quick and reliable solution. Its guarantees the protection and provides unlimited confidence. Wrapped in its security it will never let him down. The problem is that it is a temporary solution without end. What could one ever offer in its place? The layer of protection reminds me of the Russian model dolls fastened inside one another with no escape or space between. The perimeters are tight and there is little movement between the layers. The shell of dolls creates a cocooned existence. Life is lived out between the divides, leaving an empty sterile void at the centre. Everything exists to protect the shells that keep others out. This protection controls everything in its path. It limits life far beyond thought and feeling. It's a prison closed in on itself, void of all movement, choice and freedom. It lives its life out in a vacuum and controls the environment in the same way in which it oppresses its prisoners. How will Ella begin to wheen Nick from the womb of his existence to experience a real sense of identity and security?

Working alongside Nick is going to be a journey of trials, and repetitive failures experienced on both sides. For Nick, addressing the immediate priority of psychotic disturbance and the simple tasks of day to day planning might be the only achievement accomplished. To minimise the attack on his present state of mind, reminding him of who he is, his achievements, skills and abilities will be essential. This might also include simple tasks of walking out everyday and managing the payment of rent. The best results Ella might ever achieve with Nick, is to give him a sense of control over the addictions he has chosen to live his life out to. In the process of this work Nick will need to adopt an understanding that life is not easy and there are going to be times of emotional pain. Life is full of pain and suffering. Therefore establishing a qualitative relationship in order to break down the barriers of thought and behaviour is not going to be easy.

Chapter 10

Conscience and Sensitivity

It's a crisp clear day with spring in the air. The crocuses add a blend of colour to the boarders of the grass in the park and there are a variety of birds assembled on the lake before us. Lucy is sat in the car with Tony. Tony has been severely beaten up. The bruising to one side of his face is the colour of black with congealed blood gatherings just under the surface of his skin. His eye is totally closed over and the whole side of his face is swollen and lies out of proportion to the rest of his features. He is listening to Lucy identifying his personal qualities and emphasising the attributes he possesses. With one eye sunk to the roof of his lid he looks at Lucy as though in shame and then looks away again unable to accept the positive comments. Lucy ignores his deflect and continues to list the attractive qualities in personality and nature. Lucy then asks him, 'is it so hard to love yourself, just a little'. His eyes fill with tears which then flow incessantly down both sides of his face.

Tony is the most sensitive and good natured character Lucy has ever had the pleasure to meet. He is the most genuine, jovial person with a true sense of charity at heart. He has a keen sense of wit and enjoys making others laugh. He loves to be liked and when he is well he is full of energy and fun. There is an unspoken kindness about Tony. His experience of his world is profound and distinct from any other person

Lucy has ever met. He is thoughtful, over polite and overall very compliant. He takes great pride in his appearance and is fastidious in the attempts to keep his environment spotless and in order. Tony has recently moved to accommodation that will meet his needs and much has been achieved to improve the quality of life he lives. With various adaptations he is now able to sleep in bed, take a shower and sit in a chair that he is able to stand from. In spite of his health he has worked hard on agreed tasks, particularly with respect to expression of thought and feeling. Despite an angst and fear of the treatment needed he has already made progress in having long overdue tests taken and at present he is doing his best to work alongside medical professionals.

It's been with much persistence, that Lucy has managed to nudge her way in to work alongside Tony. They've been working together now for eighteen months in which time they have faced many crisis. The most alarming factor that Lucy has been the sometimes disabling responses given by professionals and others. She is sure that this must be due to a lack of knowledge, understanding and the pressure of time. No one seems to have precious time to address the complexities of such cases. Instead these cases are left until it becomes a necessity to react, sometimes only in an emergency. It must be draining for professionals who set up or organise care with the amount of paperwork needed particularly when the patient decides to pull out at the last minuet. Tony has been rushed into hospital on several occasions and trying to manage his stay in hospital has been a nightmare. As soon as he has regained consciousness and enough strength to dismantle intravenous drips, he is off home without completing treatment. However it's just great when you meet up with those medics and others who take Tony's care in their stride and allow him to pace himself around the care given. Their attitudes warrants choice and permission for those patients who cannot get it right first time. Care must surely take preference over paperwork and job satisfaction if it is to become flexible enough to address unmet need.

Tony has severe liver damage as a result of drinking alcohol. His stomach is like a round ball and so swollen that it pushes his navel inside out as though pregnant with child. He suffers from exhaustion and his mobility is impossible when his legs swell. His prognosis is not good and despite warnings of fatality he continues to drink alcohol. He has a history of self abuse and has led a somewhat sad and desperate existence. Tony has a way of either pushing you away at the same time as drawing upon every drop of attention given. His scarred arms tell his story. Past repetitive cutting is so deep that it has made an indentation into formation of both arms. When under stress he regularly sits in his arm chair with a carpet blade to hand. Its on these occasions Lucy reminds him of other means by which he can vent emotion however with a smile to the side of his face he touches the carpet blade and replies, 'just in case'. Tony tells Lucy that cutting releases the overwhelming emotional pain felt. He says, 'when I am feeling out of control I begin to cut. It releases stress and tension that might otherwise send me over the edge. If I cut to satisfaction then I can feel immediate relief. My body is attuned to its chemistry from the sense of numbness to a sensation of release.'

In stress the urge to repeat this pattern is overwhelming. If the pain guarantees a relief of connectedness and release then it has the same effect as any other addiction. In the instance of self harm the body becomes addicted to the physical biochemistry reaction of the body. A more useful term for self harm might be referred to as the 'biochemistry of addiction.'

The pattern of this self abuse is evident even within the relationships that Tony has with his drinking companions. On many occasions he has been the target and victim of some very viscous attacks within the group. This is not the first time that Lucy has sat with Tony after having had a severe beating. But this time Lucy is very concerned due to his frailty in health. Tony clings to one particular friendship that is very destructive and the aggression now outweighs his ability to protect himself. It's a rebounding enmeshed affair that has many pay offs in respect of Tony's pattern of self harm. This recent incident has shaken Tony to the core of self. Present symptoms of trauma are evident and demanding a different sort of intervention and attention. Disturbing thoughts of love, hate and paranoia menace his existence as he sits there in an alerted state of high anxiety. He looks at Lucy with his eyes hung in shame and then advises her that he needs sectioning because he thinks he is going mad. He continues to question her about his sanity and goes on to describe an embodied force of strength and evil that lives within. He tells Lucy, 'I can't let him out otherwise he will kill someone. He's inside me behind bars. He's pacing up and down thinking how he can get out. He keeps pushing himself up against the cage and attempting to squeeze through the bars. Tony expresses, 'It's taking all of me to keep him inside. Although I know he's able to protect me I fear him with all my life because I know the extent of his destruction. He has never been as present as he is now. I hate him and keep him hidden at all times. I am ashamed of him because he's not part of me. I hate me when he comes into view. I constantly talk to him to keep him inside. I would never recognise the me that I am, if he were ever to take control. That's why I need the carpet blade near me. I can then just let him out a little at a time.'

The anguish on his face tells Lucy the desperate struggle that is present. Then without warning floods of tears flow as he falls back into a mode of depression. 'What am I going to do if I can't keep him in?' Tony describes with such clarity a something or someone living within him. It's someone or something that he does not recognise as being himself. He is fearful of him and unable to quench or control the force of aggression it holds. This alter ego has promptly taken up the role of protector and aggressor. Its presence is persistent and will not leave him alone. The positive gain to this personality is that it is forcing Tony into submission of keeping himself safe, protected and away from environmental stress. Tony has become troubled and anxious about its presence and believes that he is loosing his sanity. So together Lucy and Tony spend much time acknowledging its existence and giving it a voice and expression. Several weeks pass by before the will of this personality is subdued and living in the back drop of life.

The relationship that Lucy and Tony have built has been based upon basic trust. It has been necessary to understand and accept the emotional pain Tony experiences and the way in which he finds it necessary to manage this. Lucy is aware that she will be tested to the hilt in this relationship. She has learnt not to overreact in crisis but to manage him to manage his own crisis at the same time giving him respect and understanding. It's been difficult to judge the balance of approach without knowing him well. In the relationship she has now acquired a sense of how much he is able to cope with before the silent attempts of suicide and cutting begins. It has also been important for her to understand the heart felt pain that presents a real threat and danger.

It has been important to see beyond Tony's symptoms in a way that attends his wounded psyche. Past abuses have been profound and have left the etchings of their aftermath. As a way forward Lucy has talked much about past childhood experiences and family life. This has not been easy. Tony remembers some vivid accounts of historical abuse. Some of the accounts are so real that it is as though it were only yesterday. He remembers his father's gambling habit, his absence in family life and his mother's attempts to survive on a shoe string budget. The struggle was relentless. Memories of family holiday and the survival of sibling rivalry are prominent. More emotive issues relate to Tony witnessing his mother being beaten and his feelings of hopeless and helplessness. Tony tells Lucy that throughout childhood he had attempted to protect his mother from abuses with little success. He holds his mother in high esteem and loves her dearly. He has shared with Lucy many stories of family affairs, rules, myths and beliefs.

Sharing the shameful events of childhood has been difficult. As a youngster Tony was sexually abused by a friend of the family however when he told he was never believed. Subsequently he felt betrayed and let down by the very adults who were supposed to protect and care for him. During adolescence Tony remembers his behaviour becoming unmanageable and out of control. As a result he was sent away to board at a residential school. It was at this school that he was sexually abused yet again, this time by a teacher. All this has left its scars of shame and deceit at heart. Lucy and Tony continue to discuss these abuses in the context of present relationships and protecting self.

Conclusion

Tony faces many situations that support the logic of his symptoms to cut. It has been a reliable and dependable means of coping. It distracts him from unbearable pain and shame. He has used this method as an indirect communication of anger and pain felt from past and present traumas. It serves him to express the disparate parts of self and the internalized aggression of his aggressors.

As Tony does not have a good prognosis there is only so much that can be achieved. And so in the relentless struggle that goes on for Tony Lucy continues to take a day at a time listening and attempting to improve his quality of life. Although Lucy and Tony have established a good relationship based upon honesty and trust she is conscious of regularly acting out the boundaries of this relationship. Lucy and Tony have much work to do identifying other strategies of how he might protect himself. Lucy believes the balance and approach of care given to Tony to be paramount. So she is careful not to rob him of the control or natural instinct to live the way he has chosen. By this she means she is careful not to steal the rights, liberty, choice or freedom away. She doesn't want Tony to runaway to die or be forced into institutional care but to choose the care he wants so that he can enjoy the grace of life left. And so Lucy lives with a sense of faith and hope at the heart of their contacts. Not with words spun away but with a strong belief and faith that Tony is in the hands of God.

Chapter 11

Abbie

In desperate angst she awaited for the court to convene. Daniel Bell they called. The door sung open and her child was lifted from his feet and paraded down a line of magistrates. Like a piece of meat in the market place she thought how they dare do this to him. Both anger and shame rushed through her whole body leaving her helpless to respond. Yielding to a sense of numbness she bowed her head and quietly wept. The court proceedings were hurried on by the clerk whilst orders and decisions were made. They had already made up their minds. Her presence wasn't required. It felt like a play played out in the absence of consciousness. She sat there broken hearted and completely alone. It took an enormous amount of effort on her part to realise what was happening. She wrestled with the limited strength left in her body to remove herself from the courtroom.

    She hung outside the building in hope that she might see her son. Just a few minutes she thought just to say goodbye. And then from the corner of her eye she saw him hand in hand with a court official. She felt her flesh fall away from her as her heart sunk to its deepest depths. Frozen in time her memory would always be of her child being led away from her by a stranger. Even words unspoken could never match the grief of sadness felt at that moment. The image tore at her flesh as she watched him climb the concrete staircase with his head and gaze turned towards her. She was drained from all emotion as though skewer had penetrated deep and dragged the cork out clean. Nothing could have bled her heart more. Removed from herself she fixed her gaze upon him until his image disappeared behind closed doors. Traumatised in disbelief she stood there still, emptied and drained. Her child ripped from the womb. One thousand and one reasons would not suffice now. Caged and caught up in the fear she began staging herself in the drama as though she were the accused. Condemned by the shadows that lingered in mind she would never escape her own condemnations. She would be subject to her own internal court of failings for the assault upon her child. Repeated torments of self blame would plague her for the rest of her life. No reprieve or privilege will be given in return. She would become her own executioner. She dropped to her knees but no tears would come. No one on earth, she thought, could have ever have experienced such emotional pain. Her heart cried out to the Gods in a desperate ploy for mercy and begged that they might take her life. But when silence fell she turned on self to scourge her flesh until it bled. The pain was so immense she went on to abuse her mind, body and soul with every drug she could find.

Still mesmerised by these moments her body begun to shake and shudder. Was this really happening to her? How she had wished that this was just a nightmare she was awakening from. She was numb of a sense of self as though her body had closed down. She had been living in a world of disbelief and had been thrown into the deepest warped sense of self denial ever. It felt that nothing would awaken her now. Many days and weeks passed by before reality started to emerge into consciousness. A sense of sorrow befell her and tears began to fall from nowhere. A sense of anger engulfed her so much so that her unheard cries rendered her silent. She began to piece together the picture of the real perpetrator and how she had been captured up into an unfamiliar world of drugs, violence and criminality. What had been the attraction to this male? Was it his mysterious mystifying and intriguing manner? Or was it the beginning of just another challenge? She had fallen hook, line and sinker into an evil, controlling and sinister world of associates and lover. Promises were given of dreams dreamt, guaranteed security for ever and a day and love that had no end. How could she go wrong? She searched her memory of the encounter with him. He told her how he had been orphaned at an early age and had experienced excessive abuse at the hands of nuns which left him alienated and lost in a world of his own. Abbie decided that she would be the one to cherish his fragmented self and repair all the hurts he had ever experienced. Yes, she would be the saviour, the healer of all his misfortunes. However, in the process she fell into his world and lost all sense of herself. Now in a world of uncertainty, danger and addiction she herself was struggling to survive. Not aware of her loss of consciousness she fell from the idealism of saviour to the depths of a victim in total abeyance and fear. Was it so obvious to her now what would happen to her as a result? Now nailed to the judgement of others and quashed by the very authorities that held up the rules she had become fodder for the Gods. Not worth the breath of her own existence she had lost everything she ever considered as precious. As the attraction of him fell quickly away she began to feel an extreme fear at the thought of betrayal. Daringly she thought of plots of revenge and murder. Her plan would be as sinister and depraved as he had bee. Held by a web of fear and a succession of abuses she began to plan her ploy of revenge. The sense of danger for her life lingered as she pondered upon the possibilities. In the process of what was to come she held on tightly to her addiction as a way of guaranteeing some sort of realness in life. Feelings were too raw to feel. Held by the security of addiction she was lost to all sense of herself, others and the world she existed in. A walking zombie cushioned and enveloped in a warm and cosy womb, a womb that guaranteed everlasting security. It felt that the vengeance for justice was just reinforced and stacked against her.

It took many years for Abbie to escape from the claws of this man. His subtle ploys in the attempt to maintain relationship were terrifying. This had gone on for months until one day he never returned. Meanwhile, Abbie was pushing the authorities for more contact with her child. Promises of her sons return were given if she were to find a two bedroom apartment. Whilst the council promised a two bedroom accommodation if her were to return. Abbie was hopelessly caught up in a catch twenty two with no movement between either authorities or council, and so the years went by. Then one day through a friend she was given the opportunity to join a group of dancers who were planning to travel throughout Italy dancing in nightclubs. Who could ever imagine that her life was about to change forever. Would she give this a chance? There was nothing to lose. Now, in a group with five other girls she began to put her whole heart into learning different dance steps and routines. Perhaps this was the break she was awaiting, to make a fresh start, to have an income and to be more independent. She would be able to afford the bus fare for contact with her son. She would be able to live a reasonable life without being dictated to by finances. Yes, this felt good. With the addiction now fading into the background she became focused upon a new goal.

On her return from Italy, and still driven by the experience of separation and loss of her son she began hunting for contracts for herself alone. With a little knowledge of agents and the resources of costume, the skill of sewing and an ability to put dance routines together she began to plan. She made contact with agents who were able to secure contracts in different countries throughout Europe. Abbie began travelling away for months at a time Belgium, Germany, France, Switzerland, Luxembourg and Japan. She was determined that she would save every penny earnt to put towards a home. However, the separation, distance, broken attachment and loss of time with her son didn't get any easier. She grieved much for him whilst away. She would send money home and at times fly him over to the destinations where she was working. She would buy him anything he wanted, except the one thing she could never buy back and that was the physical closeness and time. She would never ever retrieve the precious time lost. She felt lost at the thought of how she might perform miracles to compensate. Angered by the emerging thought s she began to wrestle with herself for a release. Wrapped up in an illusion to soothe and solve she turned her thoughts to the distraction of purchasing a home. This promised palace that would reunite them. It felt like an impossible mission at first but once the plans of contract started to emerge she began to rest in a tide of change. Over the months the capital started to accumulate and she became more confident about her quest. And then after seven years of travelling she had managed to save enough money to return to England to fulfil her dream.

Abbie went on to purchase a house and settle down together with her son. Her son was now fourteen years of age. Abbie was so very proud of him. Everywhere she went he would be on the tip of her tongue. He would get so very embarrassed of the overwhelming pride she exhumed. He was a very reserved deep thinking child who didn't express his emotion easily. His caring attention for others was evident particularly in the allegiance of friendships. He was easy to get on with, adventurous and fun loving. However, it wasn't easy settling down together on a twenty four hour a day basis after such a long separation. It took time to get to know one another all over again. Abbie didn't waste much time in instigating court proceeding s to revoke the order that still bound him over to the authorities. She was ecstatic when the order was revoked. What more could she have ever wanted. Free now to be with him without threat or fear. She thought back to some of the unjust, bizarre decisions made by social services whilst he was in care. One occasion she remembered well. It was just before Christmas and after she had spent some time in hospital when a quick decision was made by the auhorities to lessen contact. The decision had no reason to it and was based upon some very ungrounded and assumed information given by a social worker. It had had a dire affect upon Abbie. This put her in an uncompromising position. She was determined that they would be together for Christmas day. She thought upon how she had stolen him from the home where he had been staying and how they went on the run up until Christmas morning in order that he could open his presents. After opening his last present she then rang the police to report herself. In response Abbie was arrested Christmas afternoon and requested to make a statement about why she had taken him. It was the most bizarre statement request she had ever heard in her life. It was statement that had remained with her up until this very day. Abbie thought upon how this whole affair must have affected her son and how traumatised he must have felt but at the time it was as though she could not think beyond what had been taken away from her due to some ridiculous and outrageous assumption made by a professional.

Since Abbie had returned home the change in her sons life had been remarkable. He appeared to settle well and was making sudden progress at school. It was probably the happiest time in Abbie's life. She couldn't believe it was happening after so many years of dancing travelling and saving every penny. Her son continued his studies at school went on to study at college, qualified and secured employment and then went on to work as a Project Manager.

Abbie is now sixty two years of age with three grandchildren. Looking back she pondered on the long drawn out years of struggle. She reflected on the loss of time and the damage it had had on their relationship. She thought upon her travels and the times of departures at train stations, air ports and how these occasions deeply moved and disturbed her. At the time it was impossible to hide the tears that were shed. Her son so young at heart and would comfort her by saying, 'it's ok mum, it will be worth it'. The guilt and shame she felt over her tears were immense. Her son was so sensitive he didn't need to see the tears wept he could just sense her despair. What was this doing to him she thought? Abbie knew that years of arduous struggle had left its scars. She pondered on the reunification and how this must have been received by her son. Why was it that he had suddenly excelled at school? Had he unconsciously put time on hold until she returned? Abbie still living in naivety and the silence of missed years never once questioned her son on the effect of this lost time and distance. It was like the elephant in the room that never got mentioned. A smoothing over of the unmentioned split and abandonment that was so very apparent. How would she have changed this story if she could? If it had been possible she would have never chosen to work away. Instead she would have fought tooth and nail for the accommodation they needed at the time. She would have hammered on the doors of the authorities until they heard. Abbie thought upon the helplessness and hopelessness that had tainted her journey and impasse. She had done it the hard way as she had always done. She never gave herself an instance of grace in the ordeal. And at what cost? It was as though the crisis had driven her and had left her with a hard emotional layer of skin to protect the sense of deep hurts. It was time to acknowledge these now. Time to look at the whole affair with openness and transparency. And so she is beginning to put together the pieces that had torn their lives apart by writing and bleeding her felt sense emotion upon paper.

Chapter 12

Concluding

How might we begin to experience another individuals world so different from our own, Is it just ethnicity, culture, religion, language, status and wealth that divides and separates us or is it the discriminating process of thought that over rules in the fight for survival and belonging.

The world is full of diversity begging us to hearken and learn from its differences. We grow in security but never learn to live through or beyond our own insecurities, fears and suspicions. We allow our own myths and stories to feed into superstitions. It's not surprising that we have deep ingrained prejudices that often hold us together at the detriment of others. It's often the unknown that petrifies and keeps others out. We tend to suffer from a lack of awareness and understanding that causes us to separate and divide without reason. We guard our petty identities to secure our belongingness when we truly only belong to the expression of God in the universe.

Life is a precious gift. It's miraculous and full of purpose. Life comes alive when we share it alongside others and when we start questioning our differences with curiosity. Why am I not like you and you not like me? It begins with us being able to challenge our own beliefs and values that have shaped understanding and being continually open to new awareness. It's only with the openness of our spiritual minds that we can become so blessed by others whom we serve. It's where the merging of colours blends its beauty as well as its potential for complement and harmony. Being open to the mix of colours, listening hard and being open to the teaching it brings. It's a place where the blind are led by the deaf and the deaf by the blind and where the lame are carried by the able bodied. Even in our different doctrines and beliefs held we can still learn from one another to celebrate our differences

For me it all starts with grace. Grace is sufficient is an all too simple statement. It's the experience of grace in the journey of life. The stepping in time with grace. Grace meets us when there is no other feasible or human way forward. With grace our souls are laid bare. It's a pregnant time of receiving before stepping out in faith. There is no other place that compares. This is where true relationship begins. It's the touch of God living through us that authenticates true relationship. Relationships that have no limits, barriers or boundaries. It is similar to the bud in season when in all splendour the petals open up in a sincerity of colour. It's when the layers of petals are pulled back revealing our nakedness and vulnerabilities. It might only be for seconds but long enough for spirit to touch spirit bringing with it joy, harmony, healing and a true sense of love. What is it that stops us sacrificing pieces of ourselves for others, be it time, love, status, position, recognition or wealth.

Many of us have been broken to pieces by non-empathic relationships and responses experienced throughout life. Some have been left fragmented and in pain from the very unifying centres of family, state and institution. We are all scarred at a deeper level than we dare to admit. In the fear of breaking open we desperately guard ourselves by creating a human corset that insulates, and holds us together. Much of the business in life pervades and robs us of precious relationships with others. Human nature such as it is, sometimes gets in the way of depth relationships. If not recognised defences can deflect, repress and rob us. Rilke's poem portrays how we hide ourselves from ourselves and from God and simply expresses openness.

> We must not portray you in King's robes
> You drifting mist that brought forth the morning.
> Once again from the old paint-boxes
> So take the same gold for sceptre and crown
> That has disguised you through the ages,
> Piously we produce images of you
> Till they stand around you like a thousand walls
> And when our hearts would simply open our fervent hands hide you.

It's sometimes only in crisis that all emotional and physical endeavours suddenly become in vain and we find ourselves chasing after the wind.

The presence of the moment brings with it clarity of colours when we breathe another breath and sense for the first time that God is in us and we are part of his creation. When for just a moment we are not affected by life's demands or expectations. When for a passing moment flesh falls away and reveals the nature of God's creation. It's the birthing of sweetness from the bitter hurts that touches and transforms hearts and healing. When for a moment healing breaks through and lies at the very heart and depth of our own splits and differences. It's where mercy kisses truth. Where righteousness lies down with peace and where the lion lies down with lamb and the lamb with the lion. At that point of breakthrough one catches a glimpse of the intentions and purposes of creation. This indescribable indwelt presence. A mix of love, mercy, grace and joy of living. When everything in its entirety that is beyond comprehension suddenly awakens to purpose, plan and timing. Creation works with what we have in hopelessness and despair. It's the opening of wounds that will heal the wounds of others if we are strengthened enough to open up to our vulnerabilities one with another.

Let me encourage you to go deeper. Don't be satisfied to stay at the waters edge wade with me out to the middle streams and urge yourself forward to be emerged and saturated in spirit, and then if we fail, together we can go back to the beginning and try again. You and me, in the true spirit of living alongside another.